ELEGY TO MURDER

A MEDIEVAL MYSTERY

PRISCILLA ROYAL

IN MEMORIUM

Christine Goodhugh
With gratitude and in sorrow

"Bell, book, and candle shall not drive me back, when gold and silver becks me to come on."

   —William Shakespeare, King John, Act 3, Scene 3 (1573-1637).

"What is deservedly suffered must be borne with calmness, but when the pain is unmerited, the grief is resistless."

   —Ovid, Heriodes, v.7

CHAPTER ONE

In the fickle light of an ashen moon, Crowner Ralf struggled to glimpse even a hint that the boat he hoped to see was approaching the shore.

His eyes ached in the salt air. Wincing with pain and annoyance, he rubbed a loose bit of clothing into the corners of his eyes, then tried to clean the sweat off his face with his hand. Impatience, however, stung with even greater ferocity than burning sweat.

Finally, he saw it.

The boat was closing in on the beach.

Slowly, Ralf raised his hand to signal his men. At last, he could catch the smugglers.

Without warning, a man with a flaming torch raced from an unseen spot close to the jagged cliffs. He waved the brand and screamed to the men in the boat.

"Now!" Ralf shouted. It no longer mattered if anyone knew the king's men were here.

His men sprang from their hiding places in the low brush, then ran and stumbled down to the shoreline.

Groaning in frustration, Ralf realized they might not reach the boat in time.

Suddenly, the man with the torch fell.

Looking behind him, he saw one of his men holding a crossbow. "No!" he roared. "I want live captives, not dead ones."

"I only meant to wound him so he would not escape, my lord," the archer cried out.

It was Warin's voice, a man Ralf knew owned more sense than most. As he looked down at the dark figures of his men charging across the sand and pebbles, he concluded that Warin was probably right to try to catch at least that felon.

All hope of capturing anyone else was gone. The boatload of smugglers had reversed direction and was disappearing with impressive speed into water too deep for his men to wade.

Cursing over yet another botched attempt to arrest these men, Ralf walked toward the one man he hoped might be able to answer at least some of his questions, the one Warin had stopped with a well-placed bolt.

Or would have been able to enlighten him about the smugglers' methods, how they came to know when to avoid Ralf and his men, or even the name of their leader, if Warin's arrow had not pierced the man in the lung and not the shoulder.

"He is still alive," one of his men said, "but I fear not for long."

Ralf knelt next to the dying man. "Your soul is departing. We have no priest. God will be kinder if you confess your sins now. As the crowner and recently shrived, I claim to be an upright man and able to hear your words, although I cannot grant absolution."

The man blinked, and the fear in them dulled.

Or was the dullness caused by the closeness of death rather than relief? Ralf had little time for questions.

"You sinned against an anointed king. Tell me the name of your leader. How came you to know I would be waiting for the smugglers here tonight?"

The man coughed.

Blood sprayed over Ralf's cloak.

"Wool," the man whispered.

"Who leads?"

"Norwich," the man rasped. "Merchant." With that, blood bubbled out of his mouth, all light in his eyes vanished, and his soul fled.

Ralf stood, clenching his fist with anger. One of the man's last breaths had been wasted. He already knew the smugglers took wool.

The king had recently placed levies on wool exports to help pay for his castle building and war debts, and this had led to smuggling. Most of the time, the men who stole from the king were clumsy in their methods, but this thieving band was clever and had avoided capture for weeks.

Warin had followed Ralf and now knelt next to the corpse. "I thought to strike higher, my lord, and grieve that I failed." He looked up at Ralf. "Were you able to learn anything useful before he died?"

Ralf wanted to curse the man for shooting into the darkness when taking an accurate aim was almost impossible. But Warin was a former soldier and had served him well since this hunt for the smugglers began. The plan to keep the sentinel from fleeing into the night, as did the smugglers, may have gone awry, but his reasons for stopping him were good.

Calmer, Ralf knew that he had at least gotten two details not known before. "You are a Norwich man?"

Warin confirmed it.

"Return. Find which wool merchant is the most likely leader of this band. You are clever enough to ask good questions, but do not endanger your own life. As soon as you learn anything of value, report to me. I shall be responsible for the next step."

Warin stood. "I will do so with diligence, for I owe you much after the error I made tonight."

Ralf shook his head. "Your skills with the crossbow are well known. It was dark and your aim was off. At least we now know the leader is a merchant and where he lives. Now go."

Watching Warin disappear into the shadows to start on his journey, Ralf felt a knot of anger tighten in his stomach. Despite all his past successes bringing felons to justice, this was one crime that had utterly defeated his best efforts.

There was no secret that he was hunting the smugglers. Someone must have been sent to watch this group of king's men, although he had no hint of who that might be. The spy was likely a local man, one who not only knew the beaches of this East Anglian coast well, but had also earned an impressive silence from his fellow villagers. Many were angered by the taxes levied on them by King Edward for wars in which few had interest. Why should they have a quarrel with smugglers, some of whom might even be kin?

Ralf knew he must catch the spy, but at least he might now be closer to arresting the head of the smuggling enterprise. Once he had the leader, learning the identity of the troublesome spy would be simple.

How many wool merchants were there in a city filled with churches built with the profits of that trade, he wondered. He wasn't a local man and could only guess, but Warin was and had the knowledge to efficiently eliminate most from suspicion. Ralf felt confident that he and his men would have greater luck spying on the activities of a few merchants than catching men in boats. The spy's usefulness would also vanish with the shift in the focus of the hunt.

As he stared at the brightening eastern sky, Ralf listened to the waves lapping at the beach with a rhythm that carried echoes of mariners sighing with loneliness. A deep sadness filled his own heart, and he was possessed by an unbearable longing that was more powerful than any desire to catch miscreants.

Dedicated though he was to the king's justice and his responsibilities as crowner, the only thing he truly wanted was for this hunt to end so he could return to his ailing wife in Tyndal village.

CHAPTER TWO

The air in the priory gardens was sweet with the fresh scent of young life.

Although the fecundity of summer lay ahead—and remained the subject of profound prayer—local farms, as well as the gardens in Tyndal Priory, were filled with eager green shoots and patches of color vibrant enough to welcome bees.

It was a time of optimism. The dark seasons were finally slipping away, taking with them the daily threats of sharp hunger and icy death. Instead, there was hope and cautious smiles among those who had broken the winter-hardened earth with plows and planted the seeds.

Yet Prioress Eleanor was neither comforted nor at peace. As she walked with her dear friend and former servant in the cloister garth, she was distracted, restless, and melancholy.

These frequent attacks of unbalanced humors had caused her to consult Sister Anne. After a thorough examination, the sub-infirmarian had found nothing wrong. Perhaps the prioress was suffering from the deprivations of a long winter, she suggested? It was a common ailment. Or, the nun suggested with more confidence, the prioress only needed time to recover from the events of last autumn, when she and her family had fled their lands in Wales during the king's war. Although they had avoided capture by raiders, the weary prioress had still found Death eagerly awaiting her in a place deemed safe.

How I wish time were the answer, Eleanor had thought as she took one of Sister Anne's herb-infused tonics. When the observant sub-infirmarian looked back at her with a worried expression, the prioress knew that her quick acquiescence had not deceived her fellow religious in the slightest.

Glancing up at the thin clouds now scudding across the faded blue sky, she knew her sadness could never be cured by a tonic. Even prayer had not eased her soul.

Perhaps nothing could.

Shaking her head to fling that blasphemous thought back at the imp who had suggested it, she realized that her companion, Gytha, was no longer at her side. Frightened that something had happened, Eleanor spun around.

Gytha stood a short distance behind. Her hand was pressed against her waist, her forehead was creased with distress, and her face was as pale as chalk.

Eleanor hurried to her. "Are you ill?"

"It is only a moment's weakness, my lady."

"Let us sit on that bench. It would do us both good to sit amidst the beauty of the garden," Eleanore replied and took Gytha by the arm. Her grasp may have been gentle, but the pressure made it clear that she would brook no argument.

As they sat, Eleanor saw how profoundly weary her friend was.

Why had she not realized this before? How wicked to become so self-absorbed in her own problems that she failed to see the greater need of this well-loved friend.

"It is so lovely here," Gytha said. "I often miss the peaceful solitude."

Eleanor was surprised by the statement. Although Gytha had been happy serving her at Tyndal, she had found her vocation as Crowner Ralf's wife and quickly blossomed with happiness after her marriage.

Eleanor began to speak, but a loud rustling in the nearby shrub interrupted her.

A large red tabby emerged with a small brown object in his mouth. With clear purpose, he strode over to Gytha, dropped the gift at the young woman's feet, then sat and waited for expected praise.

Eleanor covered her mouth and laughed.

"How thoughtful, Arthur!" Gytha clapped her hands together, grinned, and bent to tenderly scratch the cat between his ears.

"A gift to tell you that he has never forgotten you saved his life," Eleanor said.

"It was you who did that." Gytha stared at the object near her feet for a long moment.

The rodent was quite motionless.

Gytha sighed with evident relief.

"I only did so because you pleaded so eloquently on his behalf." For just an instant, Eleanor was transported back to when she was a frightened twenty-year-old who had just been given the leadership of this priory by King Henry III. Not only was she inexperienced, her appointment had overruled the wishes of the religious who had chosen an older and knowledgeable woman for the position. Saving a thin kitten at the request of a tenderhearted servant girl had been one of the easiest decisions she had had to make.

The now adult cat sat before them and purred with a rumble that would have suggested ominous thunder had it not been for the love it expressed. Eleanor had named him Arthur for his regal bearing and because she loved the legends of that ancient king.

"We are grateful for your gift, sweet sir," Eleanor said to the cat, then bent closer to his ear. "I think Sister Matilda needs you to patrol the kitchen."

"Or else your lady of the moment longs for your attention," Gytha added with a chuckle.

Arthur looked from one woman to the other, rose, stretched, and ambled down the path in the general direction of the kitchens. Whether it was to attend to his duties in ridding that place of vermin, or because he knew the nuns would reward his charm with food, was a question better left to those who could read the complex minds of felines.

The moment the cat had disappeared, the brownish object at Gytha's feet opened its beady dark eyes, leapt to its feet, and, with impressive speed, fled in the opposite direction.

"We mustn't tell Arthur," Gytha whispered.

"I'll say, quite truthfully, that you enjoyed his gift," Eleanor murmured back.

After a brief silence, both knew the moment for jests was over. Eleanor put a hand on Gytha's arm. "You are ill, yet you said nothing to me. Have you seen Sister Anne?"

"I have not fully recovered from my recent miscarriage, my lady. The heart's grief and the body's suffering linger. I need only God's consolation to speed the healing."

"Does Ralf know you are unwell?" Eleanor was aware that Gytha's husband was hunting smugglers on the East Anglian coast some distance away.

"There is no reason to summon Ralf. I explained to him what I have just said to you."

Eleanor frowned. "It has been some time since your sad loss. I fear your body has been damaged far more than your spirit."

Gytha looked away, but not before Eleanor saw the tears.

She put her arms around the young woman and pulled her close. "What is it, Gytha? I can see that you are suffering more than grief over the lost babe, hard though that is. You have lost weight. Your skin has lost its rosy glow." She fell silent and simply held the trembling woman.

Gytha wept until the tears eased enough to speak. "I am ashamed, my lady."

"There is nothing you cannot say to me. Have you not always known that?"

Looking up at Eleanor, Gytha continued with a weak smile. "I am far weaker than I was when I lost the last babe. After three birthings, I have now miscarried twice. Sister Anne warned me that a third loss was more likely were I to quicken before I regained my strength. And that strength is not returning."

Eleanor felt it was wisest to say nothing.

"God has been gracious enough to make me fertile. Both my husband and I are most grateful, for we love each child with whom we are blessed, yet I cannot suffer another babe's death." Gytha sat back and took her time continuing. "Do not misunderstand me. I am truly happy to bring more souls into the world, as is Ralf." Now words failed her, and she looked away.

"Speak what is in your heart. We are all sinful, being descended from Adam and Eve, but you have never owned any dark wickedness, my child. If your thoughts are in error, we shall seek guidance and enlightenment. God does not condemn the honest seeker of truth and virtue."

Gytha looked down as if she could not look Eleanor in the eye. "Why must I quicken so often?" Her voice was almost inaudible. "This last time cursed my body with great suffering. Sometimes I struggle to rise in the morning. What is worse is that I have begun to shrink from lying with my husband, and Ralf fears our coupling too. He confessed that he could not endure life if I remained this weak and died in another birthing or if some deadly foulness grew in me after another miscarriage." She grasped Eleanor's arm. "That is my sin. I want to lie with my husband, yet I dread both a babe's death and my own because I cannot regain the strength to bear another."

Eleanor closed her eyes. The Church had long accepted St. Paul's begrudging concession that it was better to marry than burn with passion. To that, the saint had also proclaimed that a husband and a wife owed each other enough pleasure in the marital bed to prevent either from finding that solace outside marriage.

Yet pregnancy was deemed a woman's lot, part of the curse that Eve must suffer for her disobedience in Eden. A woman's only salvation was in the pain of birthing or in perpetual celibacy. That otherwise virtuous women often died in childbed occasionally caused the bereaved to ask God if death were not too great a penance. Yet the

Church had decreed that any attempt to avoid bearing children was a grievous sin, a defiance of God's will.

Eleanor said none of this to Gytha. Her friend knew it all as well as she.

"And there is another problem both Ralf and I have discovered," Gytha whispered. "His daughter, Sibley, whom I love as if she had come from my own womb, has recently grown distant and no longer laughs. My husband and I both know why."

Eleanor felt a sharp pain in her heart. "As do I, my child. She loves you and fears you will die as her own mother did." She understood the child well. Eleanor's mother had died a horrible death in childbirth, a grief that remained raw almost three decades later.

"And thus I long for a remedy that will allow me to remain with Sibley until she is a woman and even stay on this earth to be a good mother to the children that Ralf and I have or may yet have." She rubbed a hand over her eyes. "It may be wicked of me, yet I cannot see goodness in taking a mother from one child just to bear another when both may die in the struggle. Neither Ralf nor I want to deny God more souls, but we long to do so less frequently!"

It was not a dilemma that Eleanor had been forced to cope with herself, although she often admitted to God that she wished she had been able to enjoy the warmth of her mother's love a few years longer and bitterly resented the pregnancy that had killed both her and the child. And so she had no answer for Gytha. If she had had time to ponder longer, perhaps she could find one that would give comfort and obey the rules of the Church.

"That is a sin easily acknowledged in confession. You will not be the first daughter of Eve to beg God to ease the penance women serve because our foremother gave Adam the apple. Midwives may have secret methods, but their ways are both sinfully foul and more dangerous to a mother's life. Only abstinence is acceptable by the Church ..." As Eleanor struggled with her words, she knew Gytha had ceased to listen.

Gytha's eyes lacked any expression. She had drawn a curtain over her soul.

Eleanor longed to help the young woman. Nothing she was saying was different from what a priest would tell her, but she knew her hesitant speech revealed her own torment and imperfect faith. She had never become fully reconciled with her own mother's terrible death. Despite her frequent confessions, her struggles to view that cruel punishment as part of a woman's lot had remained unsuccessful.

Gytha finally gently smiled. "You are right, my lady. As Ralf and I both know, that is a question best answered by prayer and a priest's advice."

Eleanor was not fooled by her friend's easy response and grieved she had failed her. And, once again, Satan's minion wickedly introduced the usual question into her mind.

If a woman was allowed to marry and have pleasure in bed, why must she face death every time she gave birth or even miscarried? Nowhere was it written, she thought, that Eve had died in childbirth, yet she was the original sinner. Why should her daughters face a far harsher penalty when the one who had committed the sin was spared? This time, she allowed her mind to hold that question an instant longer before banishing it.

Gytha stood. "And I feel much stronger after this rest and the gift bestowed on me by darling Arthur, even if the gift seems to have found breath again and fled."

Eleanor accepted that the confidence and discussion were over and rose as well. Taking Gytha's arm, lest she be weaker than she claimed, Eleanor walked on with the young woman along the cloister garth path.

After a few moments, Gytha asked in a carefully cheerful tone, "Have you heard that Signy and her foster son are quarreling? It seems such discord is common when boys reach his age." She laughed. "I am memorizing this lest our own Fulke follows the same path..."

CHAPTER THREE

The sun eased its way through the gaps in the shutters and advanced through the room to cast warmth across the face of the sleeping lad.

Nute blinked at the unexpected brightness, then leapt from his bed with a vigor fueled by horror. Dashing water over himself, he shook like a dog and ran out the door—right into the bent-over carpenter who was examining a portion of wood for dry rot.

The man, hired by Nute's foster mother to do repairs on their house, stumbled forward but caught himself before he fell, facedown, into the gravel.

"Oswin! I beg pardon!"

The carpenter righted himself and grinned. "No matter, lad. I'm not so old my bones can't take a little jolt." Then he added with a look that suggested sympathy, "I heard your mother is looking for you."

Nute groaned.

"Up late, were we?" The carpenter winked. "I hope she was worth Mistress Signy's wrath."

Nute covered his eyes. The sun hurt. "It was no lass, nor too much ale with friends of whom she would not approve," he added in a tone that begged for trust.

"Nothing else to shame your mother, then? Even in the short time

I've been in this village, I've learned she is a good woman and well respected for her kindness."

"And I swear on that deserved reputation that I have done nothing of which I am ashamed." He set his jaw. "Nor should she be either!"

With his gray eyes half-shut, Oswin studied Nute just long enough to make a guilty person squirm with discomfort.

Nute felt like a mouse under the gaze of a hunting cat, but he returned the carpenter's examination with a steady gaze. He liked Oswin, but there was something about the man that occasionally made him uneasy.

Although quiet, the man was cheerful enough, and his middling height plus slender build suggested no threat. But Oswin's features were masked by a thick beard and long black hair streaked with gray, making it hard to read his expression. He was a hard worker, much praised for his careful craftsmanship by Nute's foster mother, but Nute had noticed how often Oswin stopped his work to look around, as if expecting to see someone he knew in a village where he was a stranger. What secrets did the man hold? Of what might he be afraid?

Nonetheless, Oswin had reacted with humor, not fear or annoyance, when Nute ran into him. This man had never offended and was often kind. Nute concluded he was simply letting unfettered imagination and worry about arguing with his mother rule his reason.

"You truthfully swear that?" Oswin's tone suggested no accusation, only the wish to be reassured.

"And on my own soul, if that satisfies you more," Nute replied, then waved at the inn. "I cannot tell my mother what I am doing because she believes it interferes with my work for her."

The man shaded his eyes and glanced up at the high position of the sun. "Aye, she might have cause to think that." He looked back at Nute and grinned. "A little late to still be in bed."

"But my task is within the king's law, and the crowner has approved." Nute might be close to fifteen summers in age, and more of a man than most of his fellows, but he still puffed out his chest like a small boy.

"There is a crowner near?"

"Crowner Ralf. He lives just outside the village." Nute wondered if he had imagined that shadow briefly darkening the carpenter's eyes.

Oswin rubbed a hand across his barely visible lips. "The sheriff's brother?"

"You know of him?" There was something in the way Oswin had asked the question that caused Nute to feel vague unease again, and yet he could not define why he did.

As if reading his thoughts, Oswin replied, "I was a Norwich man before I left to work on ships in the south, where coin was said to be more plentiful." The beard around his mouth twitched. "All of us in Norwich knew that Sir Fulke's brother, Ralf, was the crowner, but I did not know the man lived here."

"We should have told you! Had you known, you could have reported the crime that forced you to stop in our village and seek work," Nute said. "He would have caught those outlaws who stole all you had earned." Then he remembered why they probably had not. "But he has been away for some time now," he added. "He is hunting smugglers."

"The loss hurt, yet, thanks to Mistress Signy, I shall soon earn enough to leave and go on to Norwich," Oswin said with a resigned shrug. "The men who robbed me have likely disappeared into the forest and are too well-hidden to hunt down."

Nute would have sworn the man was oddly relieved.

A silence fell, and Nute's mind returned to what he must now face. He looked at the inn and sighed. He dreaded seeing his foster mother.

"Shall I go with you, lad? I could explain that I required your help?" Oswin waved vaguely at the wood he was replacing. "I can apologize, saying that I didn't know she needed you until you mentioned it, but that I was most grateful for your skillful assistance."

"You needn't lie," Nute replied but couldn't keep the relief out of his voice.

"Look over there at the base of the steps. Do you see rot?"

Nute was confused by the sudden request but walked over and studied the area closely. "I see none."

"Then my repair was successful!" Oswin laughed. "I don't need to lie, lad. You have just helped me."

What doubts he had felt about the man instantly fled. Nute grinned with delight.

Gesturing to the inn, the carpenter joined him, and they walked the short distance in companionable silence.

Nute went ahead and peered through the open door, then beckoned Oswin to follow. "She is just over there." He pointed to Signy, the innkeeper, near the entry to the kitchen, talking to the perpetually red-faced cook. "Follow me, and she will be less likely to scold if you are with me."

He went inside.

The carpenter followed close behind.

Suddenly, Oswin stopped and touched his shoulder. "Nute," he said, his tone urgent but oddly hushed. "I cannot go with you."

Confused, Nute turned around.

Despite his tan, the carpenter had turned pale. Turning so his back was to the inn patrons, he edged closer to Nute. "I see how busy your mother is. I do not want to interrupt her. Her anger with you will increase if I take more of her time with explanations."

"Her ire will come before anything she has to tell her cook." Nute urged the carpenter to come with him. "Please come!"

Oswin shook his head. "Nay, lad, I know my place. Tell your mother what we had agreed upon, then add that she should talk with me when she is free to do so. I promise to support you as I vowed, but..."

Without completing his sentence, the carpenter hurried out of the inn. As he fled, he kept his head bowed. His long hair swung down and further hid his face.

Nute stared. Although the summer day promised to be a hot one, and Oswin had been working in the heat, the youth realized that the carpenter had only now begun to sweat. The reek was pungent, not from honest labor, but with fear.

"Nute!"

He winced at his mother's tone. If scolding had claws, he was about to be ripped apart. The innkeeper might be considered a saint by the residents of this village for her quiet charity and humble virtue, and he loved her as if she had borne him in blood and pain, but she brooked no disobedience either from her inn staff or the two children she loved with the ferocity of a mother bear.

Knowing he must pay for his sins, he gritted his teeth, squared his shoulders, and walked toward her.

CHAPTER FOUR

From the entrance to the nuns' quarters, Eleanor watched Gytha walk home along the path that passed by the great priory mill. The young woman's pace was painfully slow.

After a few moments, Eleanor turned to look at the unadorned stone walls of the monastic quarters and the high walls that encircled the priory grounds.

Priory walls were supposed to keep the monastics safe from the worldly temptations and sins without, she thought, but they had never protected anyone from the havoc brought on by themselves.

"You are a sinful, weak, and selfish woman!" she muttered, looking down at her hands as if they had offended.

Nothing had been right after coming home last autumn from the English village on the Welsh border. Since her return, she had struggled to properly direct, inspire, and organize the labors of her monastics as duty required. Her usual enthusiasm for leadership lacked its former vigor.

In fairness, she had found difficult problems waiting when she rode through Tyndal's gate. Prior Andrew, a man on whom she depended to profitably manage the priory assets, was suffering rapidly deteriorating health. His leg, never fully healed from an old battle wound, had grown more painful. There was an ominous smell of decay about him, and he rarely left his quarters. When he did, two lay brothers stood near to assist him in what had become the torture of walking.

Gracia, who had been rescued by her and Brother Thomas six years ago, was ready to take vows. That would be a joyous occasion, but Eleanor knew she must find another young woman to serve her. Although Gracia had insisted she remain a lay sister and stay by her prioress's side, Eleanor's eldest brother had donated a dowry sufficient to allow this well-educated and intelligent young woman to become a choir nun. There might be no reason to prevent Gracia from continuing as Eleanor's servant, but Eleanor believed her intelligence and talents would be better used in other ways.

And then there was Brother Thomas....

Eleanor fought for control, but, with no one nearby to see her weakness, she gave into grief. Tears flooded down her cheeks. Even the hot air could not dry them before they darkened her robe with the signs of anguish.

Despite hours of prayer every day, she had been given no divine guidance on how to cope with the knowledge that her beloved monk had committed a terrible wickedness last autumn. Although Eleanor had educated herself on the Church's increasingly grim position on sodomy, she still believed in God's forgiveness.

Why wouldn't He show mercy to a man who had served Him well and was respected for his wise counsel and gentle compassion? These virtues were not imagined. They had manifested themselves countless times in the many years he had served at the priory. Nor did she even know to what degree Brother Thomas had committed the sin. Would those details not make a difference?

The arguments she held with herself were constant. She endlessly debated a question to which she feared there was no answer—or certainly none of which she was capable of comprehending. Some days, she felt as if she were a cat chasing its tail, an object that could never be grasped. Even her Arthur had ceased to do this as a kitten and thus proved himself wiser than she.

Once back at their priory, Eleanor had expected the monk to seek Brother John, now the Hermit of Tyndal, and confess what had actually happened. Since the hermit was also her own confessor, she trusted his judgment about any penance due and that he would blend firmness with compassion. Whatever decision he made as a priest would give her confidence that God's will had been served. Even if the penance required did not give her the complete peace she longed for, it would at least provide resolution and stop the endless arguments in her heart.

But Brother Thomas had inexplicably failed to seek the man out. Instead, he had spent hours on his knees in the chapel or at the window of the Anchoress Juliana. Once Eleanor would have been jealous, but she no longer suffered that particular sin. Juliana lovingly embraced the demands of her severe vocation, and Brother Thomas was renowned for rejecting the temptations women offered. Holy though she might be, Juliana was still a woman. So why had the monk not sought a priest's counsel, yet continued to beg advice from the anchoress?

Nor had the guidance seemed to help. The monk's bright auburn hair had not grayed, but his flesh had. His features had grown sharp, like those of an old man approaching death, and Eleanor had seen his once strong hands trembling. She even doubted he ate enough to keep a sparrow alive. Had he begun to fail in his duties to the priory, she might have felt justified in speaking to him, but he had not.

The only thing lacking in him was joy.

She selfishly longed for his company, not because of the lust she still felt for him but because his wit and intelligence gave her a more chaste pleasure. And she was not the only one who missed the comfort he brought with his kindness. Others had commented on his long retreats into the solitude of the dark chapel. His dazzling smile might appear when required, but melancholy lurked behind the warmth.

"My lady?"

Eleanor froze at the unexpected voice behind her and immediately put her hands on her cheeks. With bitter amusement, she noted that her tears had dried and her wicked pride was safe. She turned to greet the lay sister with courtesy.

"You have a visitor who begs a private audience," the woman said. "He comes from our regular vintner in Norwich."

Eleanor was puzzled. In the past, when the vintner's man came on his regular visits to replenish the priory cellars, Prior Andrew had discussed quantities and types of wine needed with him. Now, with the prior's poor health, she had assigned the cellarer to do this. Why was that practice insufficient now?

She had cause to worry. Master Durant had often come himself to visit with her and Brother Thomas because of the past the three shared, yet for almost a year he had not done so. Did this sudden request by his messenger for a private audience bode ill?

She nodded to the messenger and hurried back to her quarters.

When Eleanor entered her audience chamber, the man turned and bowed.

She answered his courteous greeting with grace, sat in her elegantly carved chair, and gestured for him to sit on a comfortable stool. Since Gracia was otherwise engaged, a lay sister came to serve. The young woman brought ale, freshly baked bread, and a fine local cheese. Once the man had been hospitably served, Eleanor tilted her head and gave him permission to state his purpose.

"I come on behalf of my master's wife, my lady. She has a mercy to beg."

Although his words had suggested nothing ominous, Eleanor felt a chill. "Is all well with your master's family?"

He blinked at the question before replying, "Mistress Durant and the children are in good health." He hesitated. "My master has suffered a great illness, but he is now recovering, for which we all offer prayers of gratitude to God."

It was his tone, not his words, that gave her little comfort, but she was unsure how to question him further. "And we shall add ours as well. Please continue."

Clearing his throat, he took a moment to swallow some ale.

Eleanor wondered if she imagined a fleeting expression of relief in the man's eyes when she did not press him for more details.

"The message from my mistress is this. Mistress Durant asks if you would accept her husband as a resident here for the remainder of his life. His family will stay in Norwich. A generous donation will be given to Tyndal Priory, of course, and the family will pay for his care."

"Master Durant wishes to take vows?"

"No, he does not, but he longs to participate as best he can in the monastic life. Mistress Durant hopes you will allow her to visit him often with the children, but she assures you that she would come as a sister to her husband, not as a spouse."

"Why not take vows?"

"I cannot answer that, my lady."

Eleanor found the man's reluctance to plainly answer troubling. Her question was a simple one. The response should be as well. Many felt the need to retreat from the world but did not feel capable of obeying stern monastic vows. Others hoped to take the vows closer to death. How a priory arranged accommodation depended on the purpose for the retreat.

As willing as she might be to accommodate a man she had cause to respect, this request could not be granted without more information. "You say Master Durant has been gravely ill, but, although he is recovering, you suggest he continues to need care. Would you please tell me more? I am sure your mistress would understand why our small priory would need as many details as possible."

He flushed.

Eleanor realized that her tone had been sharper than she intended.

"Mistress Durant knows the burden she is begging you to take on," he said. "Her husband joins her in apologizing for the want of detail she sent with me. I can only further say that my master remains in need of medical care and assistance in his daily life."

Eleanor was annoyed yet felt guilt over her reaction.

It was true that the priory was small, and this request did not just involve finding space for a residence on monastic grounds but providing personal care, the nature of which was unclear. The messenger came with too few details, and wasn't it unreasonable to expect her to make a decision without knowing more?

Or, she asked herself, am I simply trying to cover up my loss of compassion along with all my other failures since my return?

The man did not seem to suspect her thoughts and now bowed his head before continuing. "My master and his wife understand that the simple message with which they entrusted me requires further elaboration and discussion. If you are willing to consider their plea, Mistress Durant begs a further kindness. Would you send a trusted person from the priory to speak with her husband so they might discuss the many other details?" He looked for his mazer of ale and drained it quickly. "Since my master and Brother Thomas are friends, she hoped he might be the one chosen."

Instead of reacting with displeasure over what might be construed as telling her what to do, Eleanor brightened and replied with warm enthusiasm. "Of course! He shall travel back to Norwich with you."

The man's eyes opened wide with surprise, then he thanked her profusely for her quick and willing acceptance of his master's plea.

She gestured to the lay sister to serve more ale, then gave her an order to summon Brother Thomas from his prayers.

CHAPTER FIVE

The road to Norwich from Tyndal Priory was an easy one to travel, despite the rolling hills in between.

The breeze from the coast kept Thomas and the vintner's man cool for a while, and the hours passed comfortably for both horses and riders. As the briny odor of the sea diminished, it was replaced by the smell of the earth and well-fertilized farms rife with pungent manure.

Originally a city man, and convinced he would never get used to what he had first called the country reek, Thomas had grown fond of the scent of the sea, albeit less of the fertilized earth. Most mornings, he paused to take a deep breath on the way to prayer with his fellow monks before the sun warmed the soil and caused it to overpower the sharp odor of the sea.

And despite being raised in a world of knights and lords, he had also found an unexpected peace in the quiet simplicity of priory life—a vocation he had not willingly chosen—and a deep satisfaction in serving a tiny woman with a strong will and a fierce longing for justice.

Or so he had until the last several months.

The events last autumn had profoundly shaken him, and now that he was entering the city where Durant lived, he felt a growing unease.

What comfort he had gained from the news that the vintner had not stopped all communication because he no longer loved him, but because he was recovering from illness, was beginning to slip away. He struggled to defeat a renewed onslaught of insecurity and regain the power of reason that was deemed a more manly response.

Thomas reminded himself that he had no cause to hold on to fears that Durant had found another to love, one not burdened by vows and a tonsure. And although his beloved had suffered a life-threatening illness, Durant was not dead. For all this, Thomas knew he should be singing God's praises, not whining.

Pulling himself away from his looming melancholy, Thomas concentrated on what he had ahead of him. He had little information on what he might discover when he arrived at the Norwich house that the vintner shared with his wife and children. But Durant was alive and had especially asked that Thomas be sent to discuss the favor requested from Prioress Eleanor. That was important.

Thomas ordered himself to find strength in that knowledge.

The vintner's man halted in the middle of the busy street and turned to the monk. "We have arrived. My master's abode is just there." He pointed to a house with a wine barrel hanging above the entrance. "I will take the horses. When you are ready to return to the priory, Master Durant or his wife will arrange for your safe journey home."

Thomas nodded and carefully dismounted. It was hard to avoid being jostled by the crowd of servants running errands, racing dogs, and small carts. His foot just missed landing on a small rodent fleeing a gray tabby.

The street was narrow but ran east to west, so the sun brightened it. The monk smiled over the wise use of light that would keep the street safer from dawn until sunset.

Sniffing the air and watching the horses being led off, Thomas mused on what odd creatures men were. When he had lived in London, he never noticed how the streets or air smelled. Now that he rarely visited any place larger than Tyndal village, he was acutely aware of the odors. Was that cloying reek from rotting wood? And despite the relative cleanliness of the street, just enough stink of feces mixed with the smell of cooking to make him cover his nose.

To distract himself from the odors, he turned his attention to the vintner's two-story wooden house.

The heavy entry door, near the front left corner, was at the back of a wide, covered area where customers could be protected from all weather, especially the larger crowds who gathered on market days. It was currently open, and the number of men entering and leaving proclaimed the business to be a thriving one.

As he started toward the door, Thomas felt his legs weaken. All the relief to which he had been desperately clinging vanished.

What if Durant only wanted to mock him? Or did the vintner plan to blast him with curses because of the temptation to lie together, a sin that had caused God to strike the vintner with that near fatal illness? Was this desire to settle in a religious house a sign that he now abominated the love they had shared? Did Durant want to come to Tyndal in order to torment him for the sins they had longed for yet never committed?

He knew none of these questions were logical. The only thing about which he could be certain was that he would only learn the full story when he went inside and spoke to Master Durant and his wife. With great effort, he banished the doubts.

As he waited for a couple of slow carts to pass, he heard a commotion nearby that caught his attention.

Across the street, a man had exited a nearby house and was surrounded by a boisterous group of well-wishers. From the cluster of armed and mounted men patiently waiting, Thomas concluded the man was going on a journey and was wealthy enough to hire considerable protection from wayside robbers.

When the friends began to disperse, the man turned and saw Thomas. His eyes widened with joy, and he cried out, "A man of God! What a wonderful omen for this pilgrimage!" He gestured for the traveling party to wait, rushed to this monk, and fell to his knees in front of him. "I beg a blessing," he murmured with a hopeful look.

"Your pilgrimage finds favor enough in God's eyes," Thomas replied, giving the gift his vocation demanded despite his own sins. As the man rose, Thomas asked, "What is your destination?"

"Bawburgh to celebrate the feast of St. Walstan."

Thomas nodded. He knew the shrine as it was not too far from Tyndal Priory. "If I am not wrong, you are a merchant," he said. "Although all saints deserve veneration, I am curious enough to ask what special reason you have to take time from your trade to honor the patron saint of farmers?"

"I want to ask a gift from St. Walstan: that he beg God for mercy on behalf of my father's soul." The man looked away. "I have been a bad son, and this is the least I can do to make up for my sins."

There is a tale here, Thomas thought and, hoping the merchant would explain further, gave him an encouraging look.

The man needed little encouragement. "He was a prosperous farmer and I his heir. When I was of an age to help him much more with the working of the land, I ran away, having no desire to plow the hard earth and sweat over harvests. God was kind, and I found a way to prosper in Norwich, but when I went back to see my father and boast of my success, he told me I was no son of his and barred the door to me."

"Did you not make peace?"

The man's eyes grew moist. "Never. When he was in danger of losing all after some bad harvests, I sent word that I would buy the land so he might remain and then pay for help so my younger brother could continue to work the farm through the evil times. No one ever replied. A few weeks ago, I received word from a villager that both my father and brother had died of a fever. The man also said that my father cursed me with his dying breath." He covered his face with his hand and turned his head away.

And whose pride qualified as the more grievous sin, Thomas wondered. The willful son or the angry sire?

"And thus I travel to the shrine and holy well at Bawburgh for my own sins and for his soul. May God forgive me for failing him. I was a thoughtless and wicked youth to so disregard my duty and disobey my father's will."

"You will surely find God's forgiveness in this pilgrimage."

"His death grieves me beyond words," the merchant replied, looking back at his house. "Not only shall I beg the saint's intercession on my father's behalf, I will give the shrine a gift as atonement for my failure of obedience."

Thomas wished the merchant well on his journey.

As the man walked back to mount his horse and begin his penitential trip, Thomas grew painfully conscious that he had many grave sins for which to atone and had been much too self-absorbed of late to properly do so. Although he would not be begging mercy from St. Walstan, he was obliged to seek a path back to God, a journey that both his vows and soul demanded.

In truth, the reason he had delayed too long was cowardice. The Anchoress Juliana did not know his precise sin, but she knew how deeply he suffered and had urged him repeatedly to seek Brother John for confession and penance. Even knowing his soul faced Hell should he die, Thomas was terrified of how painful and lengthy the penance would be.

The carts had passed. The pilgrim had left on his journey. Brother Thomas knew this task required by his prioress could no longer be postponed.

He crossed to the vintner's house, eased his way past the customers gathered outside, and walked through the door.

CHAPTER SIX

There was a room on the right, immediately inside the house.

Thomas stood to one side to let some men go by and then looked in.

A large window extended across one wall and not only provided good light to see the wines but could be opened on market days and thus serve a greater number with efficiency. A journeyman was discussing wines for sale to a man whose dress suggested he served a wealthy family. Just behind that customer, Thomas saw worn stone steps leading to the cellar, where he assumed the barrels of wine must be stored.

Glancing up, the journeyman started when he saw a tonsured man. "Brother! How may I help you?" He politely asked the buyer to wait a moment while he spoke to the new visitor.

"I have been summoned by Master Durant and his wife," Thomas replied.

"You are Brother Thomas from Tyndal Priory?" The journeyman's smile was welcoming.

When Thomas bowed his head in acknowledgment, the man summoned a young lad and told him to take Thomas directly to Mistress Megge.

The woman who greeted Thomas at the back of the long hall was plain of face and in her attire, suggesting she was of little status and even less wit.

But Thomas was well aware of how first impressions deceive the superficial observer. Distracted though he might be with fear, grief, and his sins, he had only rarely been that kind of fool. First, he knew that few of humble state, even servants close to the king, wore robes of such fine cloth. Second, he noted shrewdness flickering in the woman's hazel eyes.

"I am Mistress Megge," she said with a smile and bowed her head with humble respect to a man of God.

The warmth of her greeting did nothing to add any fashionable beauty to her face, but it did reveal gentleness and suggested a kind heart.

Thomas liked her.

She steepled her hands as if in prayer, then asked him to follow her into a small dining hall.

There was just room for one trestle table with seating and a small oaken table to hold any plate or vessels needed for simple family meals. Closest to the wall was a short bench big enough for a couple of smaller folk, probably children, or one adult. On the other side of the trestle were two chairs, most likely for the vintner and his wife.

"We are honored by your visit." She gestured for him to take one of the chairs.

"I am the one honored by your hospitality," Thomas replied, his words honestly meant.

"As you have likely been told, I am Master Durant's wife."

"He has spoken of you often with profound love and respect." Thomas noted she had left the door ajar out of respect for his vocation. Just across the hall, another door opened into a well-trimmed and sunlit garden, which he assumed also had the luxury of a latrine. The kitchen was also probably outside to keep the house safe from any fire.

With a modesty that still owned nothing of cunning, she responded to his courtesy, and then went to fetch both wine and sustenance herself.

When she placed the offerings next to him, she said, "In order that we may have some time to speak before you see my husband, I told our servant to take the boys off and continue teaching them to fish." Her brief laugh was filled with love. "They are good lads but boisterous. I fear we would have little time to speak in peace otherwise."

Although he might have wished to see his godsons, he knew her decision had been a wise one. If their father remained in grave health, the boys probably also needed a day of distraction from their fears for his life.

"Having been a lad once," he said, "I understand the appeal of learning how to net my own dinner fish. Now that I am a man, I can appreciate how a parent might pray for a few hours of peace!" His mother died early, but the cook who raised him often shooed him off in the company of another servant so she could prepare food for the noble table without a boy tugging on her sleeve and asking interminable questions.

Mistress Megge sat, folded her hands in her lap, and waited for him to partake of what she had offered.

He took the wine and sipped, noting that she had served him a fine vintage when others might have given a rare guest, especially a religious, one of lesser quality. But he also understood that she wanted a moment to study a man she had never met but one who was clearly of great importance to her husband. Once again, he did not make the mistake of assuming that this quiet-mannered woman, who could fade into the background of any company, lacked perception and cleverness. This scrutiny did not trouble him, perhaps because he had concluded she was inclined to compassion in her judgments.

"You know of my husband's desire to retire to your priory for the remainder of his life, that he does not wish to take vows, and that he will need ongoing care due to his ill health?"

He appreciated her directness. "Prioress Eleanor relayed all of the message sent to her, including your request that I be the one to come here for further discussion."

"Then I shall tell you what I must before you see my husband."

He felt a chill and hoped she did not see him shiver despite the warm air.

"My husband and I are of one mind in this decision. There is no discord between us, nor do we seek to abandon our marriage vows."

Thomas nodded.

"I emphasize the latter because our priest said the Church might grant us the right to annul our marriage were we to offer gifts to God's glory as recompense for the mercy. But we have decided there is no reason to do so. Vows are sacred to us both, and we are content to continue the marriage as brother and sister only." She held up her hand. "It is my husband who must explain this further, Brother, but I had to assure you myself that this state is one in which he and I are of one heart."

Questions were overwhelming him, but Thomas knew he must let her continue.

"I might have joined him in residence at your priory to ease the burden of his care on your monastics, but we have two children. It is my duty to stay here in order to raise them to manhood, if God is generous. And I must prepare them to take over this business or, in the case of the younger, perhaps enter into another trade. Our oldest, Thome, is only five, but he is bright, eager, and takes after his father. Even if it does not take him long to learn the vintner trade, he obviously has many years before he becomes a man."

He murmured understanding.

"Until that time, I hope to visit my husband with our sons at Tyndal Priory on a frequent basis. Should God grant me life beyond my duty as a mother to raise our lads, I might take vows and retire from the world but not at your priory. If my time on earth is longer than that of my beloved husband, I would prefer to be cloistered nearer our sons. During my visits with him, however, I will do all I can to ease the hardship of our presence on your generous hospitality. But he loves his sons, and seeing them will strengthen his health."

"Your concern for us is most thoughtful, mistress, but Prioress Eleanor said that you planned not only a generous bequest, but to pay for your husband's care. That will allow us to attend to the needs of his health, yet I do not know the state of that nor the exact care he will require…"

"Details he will soon tell you himself, Brother. My purpose in meeting with you first was to offer you sustenance after your journey, assure you of my complete concurrence in this decision and of my ongoing devotion to my husband."

How sad she now looked, Thomas realized. Whatever brought about this sudden request by Durant to live out his days at Tyndal, he saw that she suffered a profound sorrow even though he believed her assurance that she and her husband had agreed to this plan.

After a brief silence, Mistress Megge stood. "It is time for me to take you to my husband. There I shall leave you both to confer in private. If either of you require anything, there is a bell in the room. You need only ring it. I shall come immediately."

With that, she led him up the stairs to a gallery between two bedchambers. The smaller must be for the boys, Thomas thought, and the other for the parents. Approaching the larger one, he smelled the pungent odor of ointments, herbs, and something unpleasantly sweet that he feared to define.

Then she opened the door, announced his arrival in a loving voice, and stood to one side.

Thomas entered the room.

CHAPTER SEVEN

Oswin could not sleep.

Even though the straw was drenched with his sweat in the loft where he lay, it remained hard enough to jab through his clothes and into his flesh. The bite hurt like the teeth in his carpenter's saw.

During the best of nights, he was often awakened by dreams filled with grinning crowds chanting for his death, the feel of a rough rope around his neck, and the screams of tortured children. This time, it wasn't gruesome night terrors but leaden reality that caused all sleep to flee.

He rose, slipped out of the inn stables, and headed toward the village square.

The air remained warm from the sun, although that had long vanished. Satan's joyless rule of darkness was well established. As Oswin looked into the night sky, tears flowed down his cheeks.

The torment of his sorrow had not abated. His wife had died of some plague. His motherless and sick baby girl had been left to starve in filth on the icy streets of Norwich. Clenching his fists, he swore with passion, a rage that had blindly driven him back to England so he might kill the man who had lied to him.

It was that man, human filth unworthy of being called one of God's creations, whom he had seen yesterday in the village inn.

Oswin uttered a cry that sounded like the howl of a bewildered animal mortally wounded in sport. Bile rose into his mouth, but he swallowed the burning sharpness rather than spit it out. He might have escaped the gallows for one murder, but he would welcome the noose this time, even as his bowels turned to water in terror, if he could kill that man at the inn.

For some inexplicable reason, a breeze from the sea now touched his face with gentleness. When he looked to the sky, the stars twinkled as angels carried their candles during Satan's hour in an effort to remind mankind that God still existed despite the darkness.

Filled with emotion that was an odd mix of anger, fear, and sorrow, Oswin forced his gaze back to the dark earth. He did not deserve that signal of hope when he planned to disobey God with such eager and deliberate joy. He had begged forgiveness for his first murder, but he would feel no sorrow over this next one. When he returned to England, he knew well that a noose awaited him, that the Devil was unlocking the door to Hell, and that he would grin with especial glee as he welcomed Oswin to eternal damnation.

The gust of air shifted direction and now brought with it the sweet scent of flowers heated during the day.

Why was God tempting him this way? For a brief instant, he felt his resolve slip and asked himself why he shouldn't become what he professed to be: a carpenter, struck by misfortune, who had been given work by a good woman in a village he found appealing. Indeed, it was all true if he omitted the reason he had left Norwich some time ago and then come here.

"If I let my anger go, I could stay," he murmured, taking a deep breath. "Surely God would let me live and atone in some way for that first crime."

But reality argued against such dreaming. Even if he could forget his dead wife and babe, the sheriff's brother, the crowner, lived here. That man knew him. The long hair, thick beard, and now gaunt face might be a good disguise for most, but Oswin knew Crowner Ralf was no dolt. And, although confident that the man in the inn had either not seen him or hadn't recognized him, he could never be sure that someone passing through Tyndal village from Norwich might not on some future day.

His longing for revenge returned and chased off the momentary hesitancy, and he was grateful it had. "I thought only Satan deluded us with the false hope of happiness," he sneered. "Must I now confound my wickedness by claiming that God is the Master Liar?"

But perhaps he shouldn't mock God. Might He have approved of his longing for vengeance? Wasn't it a sign that his quest had merit when he found a man in a French inn who not only told him of the fate of his family, but led him to a sea captain who would, for a fine price, take him back to England?

He first clenched his fists with determination, then lifted them upward as if trying to rip the candles from the angels' hands. If he were to succeed in his plan for revenge, he did not want this reminder that God longed for men to follow a more virtuous path. He needed the Devil's darkness...

The first blow on the back of his head only stunned him.

The next ones were harder, crueler, and meant to break him—as they did after darkness took possession of him and he felt no more pain.

Nute had just finished circling the village as the crowner's night watchman when he heard a cry from the square. Knowing this boded ill, he tightly gripped his cudgel and raced there. In the quiet of a sleeping village, his running feet were as loud as the hooves of a horse carrying a messenger with bad news.

Although there was some light from the moon, Nute saw only a disappearing shadow as he entered the square.

"Stop in King Edward's name," he shouted.

But the shadow either had no desire to honor the king's law or had never existed. Nute briefly wondered if he had imagined seeing anyone.

What was real, however, was the body lying just a few feet away. Tempted though he was to chase the perpetrator, Nute chose to ignore a creature who might be imaginary, or more certainly had safely escaped, and drop to his knees beside the victim.

Was the motionless form dead or did it still possess a soul? He reached out to touch the body.

It was Oswin.

The man might be bloody, but Nute realized he was still breathing.

The unaccustomed uproar had caused a few men to leave their damp beds and damper wives, peer out of windows or doors, and see what the commotion was all about. Some, in various degrees of undress, began to gather in the square.

Nute jumped up and went to that small crowd.

Clutching one man by the shoulder, he gestured to the road leading to the priory. "Run to their hospital, tell them that our carpenter has been severely beaten, and bring a lay brother back to tend him."

Then he grabbed three others by their arms and pulled them to the now groaning Oswin.

"Stay on guard over him while I fetch my foster mother. If he can be moved, we four can either carry him to a place in the inn at her direction or to the hospital. The rest of you, go home to your beds. In the morning, you will learn all there is to know."

With that, he ran to awaken Signy.

Had Nute stopped to think about it, he might have been both surprised and proud that men, far older than he, had accepted his commands without question and quickly obeyed the orders of a youth.

CHAPTER EIGHT

"You will probably live."

The lay brother from the hospital finished bathing the carpenter's head wound with what smelled like wine and swiftly tied a herbed-filled poultice against it. Then he checked the rib area.

Oswin winced and grunted.

"You did not scream," the lay brother said with a brief smile. "Maybe a bruise? A crack? Be careful of it, but God may have protected you when you were kicked."

A man standing nearby whispered to another. "I heard it from a holy man that the priory hospital washes wounds with the same wine that Our Lord created at Cana. God has deemed the infirmarian, Sister Christina, to be so holy that He regularly sends supplies to her."

"And I have heard that they cleanse wounds with holy water," a second replied.

A third considered this for a moment. "Aye, well, both are likely true."

The lay brother rose from where he had knelt on the inn floor and wiped his forehead. The morning air was already shimmering with the promise of another hot day.

"He has a broken head and several wounded ribs," he said to those gathered around him. "I cannot judge what other damage was done inside him, so do not think it wise to carry him as far as the hospital. The jolting might kill him."

"He shall have a bed and quiet very near the inn if it is safe enough to carry him that short distance," Signy said. "I have empty space where I used to live before my uncle died." She gestured in the direction of the kitchen. "It is just through there and to the right."

The religious smiled. "That is possible, if he is as carefully moved as he was to the inn floor, but he also needs someone to care for him until he is healed or can be taken to the hospital."

"There is a good widow who would welcome some extra coin," Signy replied. "He may stay in my old hut for as long as necessary. Oswin is working for me, and he is a fine craftsman." She looked around the small group and smiled. Her comment about his carpentry should be bruited about if he wished to stay longer than her own need of him required.

The lay brother watched her with admiration. He knew from whom the coin would come for Oswin's caregiver, as well as who would pay all other costs. "Sister Anne will visit to see how he is healing, or else she will send someone whom she deems competent to oversee treatment."

"When can we move him?" Nute had remained silent after his foster mother arrived. The briefly authoritative man had reverted back to the modest youth. Facing his mother's wrath had become too frequent, and he could almost recite what she would say to him once they were alone.

Signy did not even glance at him. "The space nearby awaits," she said to the lay brother. "I have already sent word to ready it. Until the widow comes, I will sit with Oswin."

Nute trembled. Her tone, suggestive to others of calm efficiency, had sharpened in his mind with her pointed disregard of him. His imagination began to increase the pain of the anticipated tongue-lashing.

The lay brother looked at the three waiting men who had helped carry Oswin inside, then at Nute. "You four will be sufficient." He pointed to the net that still lay under the carpenter. "That is strong enough to hold him, but you must walk carefully." He looked at Signy. "Is there a way out that lacks any step?"

She gestured toward the kitchen and then at Nute. "You shall accompany me," she said to him. "I will summon a fourth to carry Oswin instead of you." She waved to a serving woman and told her to bring a man from the stables.

The lay brother directed the four men as they slowly raised the carpenter from the floor.

"Walk softly at the same pace if possible," the lay brother said, and the innkeeper led them through the kitchen.

As they approached the hut outside, Signy opened the door, directed them to the waiting bed, then held out her hand to keep Nute from entering.

He stumbled backward, just catching himself before falling. All hope of retaining manly dignity was lost.

Signy took him by the arm and pulled him farther from the door. "You may now explain what you were doing wandering the village in the middle of the night."

Nute remained speechless. His work for the crowner, a source of pride and honor to him, now withered to a pathetic triviality under the glare of his foster mother.

"Was it a woman?"

He rapidly shook his head.

She gestured with contempt at his club now resting against the inn wall. "And how do you explain that wretched piece of wood?"

"I have done nothing wrong."

"You have not earned the right to be the judge of that."

"No, Mother." He prayed that the sun would be kind enough to allow a shadow to obscure his face and hide from her how close he was to tears.

"Drink, was it? Fights? I do not know many such wicked lads in the village, but I am so busy tending the inn by myself that I do not have the leisure to learn of such things." She tilted her head and gazed at him with such fury that the look alone could have burned an entire cow to a crisp, let alone one youth.

He began to weep.

"Speak, lad. The speed with which you summoned help and called for me suggests the acts of a man, even if your continuing failure to assist me, as you should, points to a willful, disobedient child."

Sobbing, Nute was incapable of hearing the softening of her tone. Signy had always listened to his side of any disagreement in the past, even when he was a child and well aware that he had erred. This was the first time he had ever felt she was being willfully unfair, and he ached from that perceived betrayal. A part of him still insisted she was right, as she was wont to be, but, in his longing to act the man, he refused to concede the possibility.

"How dare I argue with a saint?" he thought and then realized with horror that he had said it aloud.

"What did you say?"

"I had honorable cause," he barked, trying to cover his disrespectful retort with an equally ill-advised aggression. "With all the strangers coming through the village from a pilgrimage, and Crowner Ralf away hunting smugglers, I have been acting as a night watchman."

"And this is why you do not wake up until long after the inn has opened and you are needed here?"

"The crowner approved my work, saying it would be of great assistance to him." How inadequate those words now sounded.

Signy raised an eyebrow. "And you, of course, explained to our Ralf that I required you to be at the inn because of the great need I had of your help."

He slammed his fist against his thigh. He fought a growing sense that he was failing the woman who had given him and his sister a loving home and one he could not have loved more if she had given birth to him.

Frustration won. Defensive anger took over. "I do not want to work in the inn. My sister is better suited to dealing with jacks of ale and bowls of stew. Let her take on more responsibility. I want to work for Crowner Ralf and bring miscreants to justice. That is a man's work!"

"It is your duty as my foster son to take over the inn. This is not a choice. You are my heir."

"Ingerith can do so. Did you not take over the inn after your uncle died?"

Signy's face was red. She took a deep breath to calm herself, and her voice dropped. "Nute, she is still too young to do more than she does. Nor can I leave her the inn when I die. It must be you."

"You lie!" Nute was horrified that he had just shouted those words, but he was desperate. "Your uncle left you the inn. You can give it to my sister."

"He knew I would not marry. Ingerith may, and if she does, it will become her husband's property. Although I pray she marries a good man, I cannot foretell that. The only way to protect her is if you are my heir for I know you will do all you can to protect and support your sister. To be my heir, you must learn to run the business, just like any other lad would a trade." Her tone had softened as had her look as she spoke these words.

Nute realized that everything she said was reasonable, but he could not give up his dream of being a king's man. Even Crowner Ralf said he had the needed skills to do well. How could he face a lifetime of serving food to strangers when he could be riding out like a knight to fight against evil men? And as a king's man, surely he could still protect his sister against anything.

"I shall never become an innkeeper," he said with a growl.

Signy didn't utter a word. All she did was look at him with a sorrow so deep it turned the air icy with her grief.

He could no longer bear this. "You can sell the cursed place for all I care," he shouted and fled.

"You can hope for that if you will, lad," Signy murmured as she watched him disappear, "but Ralf owes me a debt or two, and he knows it well."

CHAPTER NINE

Had Thomas even wished to do so, he could not have recalled a single moment after his departure from the vintner's home in Norwich to this moment when he stood in Prioress Eleanor's chambers. His last memory was holding Durant in his arms as they both wept over a sorrow that would remain in their hearts until Judgment Day.

"Master Durant was castrated," Thomas announced in a voice far stronger than he believed himself capable. "He lives, but his health is poor. He believes he has little time left on earth."

Prioress Eleanor uttered a cry. "How did this terrible thing happen, Brother? Why did he not send word? We could have cared for him."

"Durant was on the king's mission," he told her. That much was true, but as he proceeded to tell the tale, he led his prioress to believe that the mutilation had been committed by the king's enemies as revenge for the vintner's discovery of their plots. "Had someone not been passing by and seen him lying in the street, he would have died." That was also true.

What he carefully omitted was Durant's usual practice of finding solace in male sex after a successful mission. The night of the tragedy, he had discovered that the man he was fondling in the darkness had a tonsure, and Durant could never bring himself to couple with a man vowed to God. When he backed away, he bumped into someone behind him who pinned his arms and covered his mouth. With mockery as cruel as the act, the tonsured man took his knife and castrated the wine merchant. The last thing Durant recalled was their laughter as he fell to the ground and knew he would bleed to death.

"He or his wife could have sent word." Eleanor's voice trembled. Her horror was great, not because the vintner was the purveyor of fine wines to the priory, but because he had become a friend.

"He did not wish it, my lady. Neither he nor his wife believed he would live long. As for coming here for care, he was too frail. Had this not occurred in Norwich, he would have died without his family at his side. The wound soon grew foul as well."

"We would have prayed for him."

That was something Durant was convinced he did not deserve. Although his wife never asked why this terrible wound had been inflicted, he had told her the same story he wished Prioress Eleanor to hear. Yet after meeting her, Thomas suspected she knew far more about her husband than the vintner realized. That she continued to love and support him was a credit to both her heart and faith in God's mercy.

"Had he died as quickly as he feared, there would not have been time to beg us for our orisons."

"Yet he has lived."

"But not, perhaps, for long. This is why he wants to retire here, under our care, so he might reject the world."

"But not take vows?"

"He feels unworthy and cannot endure the requirements of monastic life, although he hopes to spend much of his time in prayer. He also has two sons whom he loves and wishes to see as much as he can. His duty as a father remains dear to him."

"And his wife?"

"Mistress Megge is a woman of rare virtue, my lady. She considers her marriage vows and duties as everlasting ones. Before I met with Master Durant, she explained that she would never marry another, even after her husband's death, and is content to remain in the union but only as his sister. It is her belief that conjugal relations are solely for the purpose of having children. They have two. She concluded that God has been sufficiently kind."

"I honor her choice and admire her reasons." Eleanor's own Aunt Beatrice had chosen vows over remarriage after her beloved husband died. Many women did prefer to avoid a second or even a third marriage.

She walked over to her window and looked out across the priory grounds. It was a view that often brought the calm of objectivity when a decision must be made. The distant tumbling of water over the mill wheel provided a muted backdrop to the songs of birds hidden within the vibrant greenery of the fruit trees in the orchard on her far right. She sighed with brief contentment and thanked God for that gift. Peace rarely visited her of late.

Turning to face Thomas, she said, "We still have our original visitor accommodations in which he may reside. With the new building, we have had little need for them, and whatever repairs are required can be easily done. I assume he will bring a servant, and there would be space for that man where Master Durant lives. When his wife and boys visit, they can share the extra room. As for care, our hospital can tend to his physical needs. Sister Matilda will confer with Sister Anne on what diet is best to maintain his strength." Her voice trailed off. As she looked at her monk, she tried to keep her expression unreadable.

Yet he knew what she had omitted addressing and now expected him to decide. He nodded his understanding of what she needed to hear from him, bowed his head, and pretended to fall into deep thought.

The moment in Norwich when Durant had begged Thomas to be the one to guide him back to God had been rife with both their worldly passion and other far more complex elements of their mutual love. How could he ever explain how important it was to them that she approve the request? Had this been a plea from a husband and a wife, it might have been easier, but there were no words to express how the earthly nature of a love between two men could also include this current chaste longing.

After Durant had told of his castration and they had dried their tears, the two men swore to bind themselves to each other for the remainder of their lives. It was then that Durant had whispered into Thomas' ear, begging him to be his spiritual adviser. Their love must now be utterly chaste, he had said, and God surely would not curse the oath they had just sworn. Durant confessed that he needed Thomas by his side as much as possible before he died. It would bring him peace.

Thomas had wanted to cry out that Durant might be free of lust, but his own body was not. Yet his love for the vintner was deeper than a longing to couple. If God would allow it, he would willingly care for this man tenderly and chastely for the rest of their time together. Any carnal union would be relegated to dreams Thomas could not control. Nonetheless, he feared that God would not allow him to be the vintner's spiritual advisor. Would he not taint any hope Durant had of heaven? Thomas believed his own unconfessed sins were that foul.

He swallowed and looked up at his prioress. "Master Durant will need spiritual care, my lady. When he and I spoke, he expressed a wish that I be the one to tend to his soul. I told him that you must make that decision." Under different circumstances, he would have suggested the choice and even volunteered himself, but he felt he had lost that right.

Eleanor said nothing.

"As you well know, my lady, I am a wicked man and unworthy of the role as his spiritual advisor. Indeed, I believe I would hinder Master Durant's journey to a holier life. Since our return from Wales, I have been praying for guidance and seeking wisdom from our holy anchoress. What I have not done is confessed to Brother John and sought the proper penance for my sins."

"That is long overdue."

With gratitude, he heard no condemnation in her tone. Taking a deep breath, he continued. "Sometimes it is hard to find the words that best express both the sins and the sorrow we feel in committing them. For that reason, I have occasionally advised a few of your nuns to seek guidance and clarity from God before confession. To adequately perform penance, I believe one must understand the severity of the sin. It is only then that we feel the gravity in our heart and can truly cleanse our souls of the evil."

"You have surely done that by now, Brother, and will visit our hermit without further delay."

He nodded.

"In that case, I shall let the decision about Master Durant's spiritual counselor rest unanswered until I know the penance you must serve." Her smile was gentle. "You and our vintner have long been friends. I know having you by his side would bring him both strength and comfort. I shall pray that God will be kind and that I may soon grant Master Durant's request."

As she fell silent, Thomas assumed the audience was over and turned to the door.

"One thing more, Brother."

He looked back in surprise.

"It seems God may again require us to serve His demand for justice."

Then she told him about the assault on the carpenter.

CHAPTER TEN

After the monk left, Eleanor returned to her window and grieved as her darkening mood banished all vibrant hues in the outside world until only gray remained.

The new life that had brought such promise to her heart a brief time ago now looked terrifyingly fragile. The thoughts of coming summer lushness filled her with unease. Surely that bold opulence was only a sign of worldly arrogance and more likely to foretell the nearness of the world's end and God's hard judgment.

She shook her head and turned her back on the window.

Yet the birds sang despite her gloom. A gentle breeze brought the scent of flowers into the room. Creation should be enjoyed, she thought, for the earth and its creatures had all been made by God. And if He had never meant men to feel joy, He would never have created so much beauty nor allowed the pleasure of the Cana marriage feast.

Suddenly, she felt a pressure against her leg and looked down.

"Nor," she said, bending down to pick up the purring red tabby, "would He have created cats."

Kissing him between his ears, she carried Arthur over to her chair and sat, allowing him to curl up on her lap. Before settling, he rubbed the side of his head on her arm. She took the hint and petted him.

"I think your sire and his lady must have passed too close to Sister Matilda's spices, especially the saffron, and gifted that hue to you," she said, admiring his intense color. Then she rested her head on the back of the chair.

The rolls of accounts sat on a nearby table and demanded her attention. She ignored them. Right now, the suffering of others took precedence.

There was her monk's torment. There was Gytha's health and Ralf's fears. There was a man beaten senseless in the market square. She took in a deep breath and slowly let it out.

As for the crime committed last night, it was not within her authority. The violence did not take place on priory grounds, nor was the man assaulted one vowed to God. Yet she knew she could not ignore it. The priory was not only the moral center of the village, it was supposed to stand for peace and God's compassion. As the king's man, Crowner Ralf might be the one responsible, but he was absent. Did she not have a duty to do something?

He was also her friend and married to Gytha, whom she dearly loved. Of course a message would be sent to him, but a swift beginning to any investigation was crucial. Ralf had often helped her with the resolution of crimes within her jurisdiction. He would be surprised if she did not do the same in return. With this in mind, Eleanor had just sent Brother Thomas to question the wounded man and Nute for details about the event while they remained clear in their minds.

The arrival of Brother Thomas to see Oswin would make the villagers feel more secure. The monk was deeply respected for his kindness and skills. Many whispered that he was a truly holy man. No husband feared for his wife's virtue in his company. No woman worried that his glance was tainted with lust.

She rubbed her eyes and groaned as she thought on that reputation.

The cat looked back at her and mewed with a concern that belied the assumption that cats were only single-minded predators.

"It is nothing, Arthur," she said and stroked his head.

How things had changed since their return from the Welsh border. Now she wished that Brother Thomas had drunkenly broken his vows and lain with some serving wench as she had feared last autumn. That was a sin, but it was one easily confessed and forgiven by priests. What may have happened, however, was far graver in the eyes of the Church. Men had been burned at the stake for sodomy. Not yet in England, she thought, but how soon before they were?

And was that horrible death even God's will?

Fear that she had offended God by asking that question made her shudder.

Yet her aunt, Sister Beatrice, had taught her that God never minded the questioning, either by men or women, nor did He mock the longing for answers. Hadn't the Apostle St. Thomas doubted the very resurrection until he was given physical proof? He was never condemned for his questioning or accused of heresy.

As for being a woman, she had never believed that being the daughter of Eve made her concerns less worthy of note. If women were truly so intellectually frail, Sister Beatrice had said with a twinkle in her eye, then God probably understood their greater need for answers.

Shifting in her chair, Eleanor looked down at her cat.

He purred.

Was it a sin to let people continue to think Brother Thomas was a holy man, perhaps even a saint, when he had committed such an egregious transgression?

Although Eleanor had never met a confirmed saint, she was aware that such holy souls were not always virtuous from birth.

Women who lived as prostitutes like St. Pelagia or St. Mary of Egypt were two examples. Even St. Paul had imprisoned Christians and acted with violence when he was still named Saul. None of these lied about their sins. Indeed, they often spoke of them to remind others that they were all imperfect creatures. The hard journeys made to God's grace were praised, not condemned.

But others, also deemed holy by their followers, hid their vileness behind false smiles and puffed chests but swiftly pointed at men and women whom they claimed were the truly vile sinners. Not only were such men disinclined to admit their hypocrisy, Eleanor suspected that some would deny it even when God pointed out their wickedness on Judgment Day.

Which, then, was her monk? He had never spoken of any tendency to sin with men, nor had there been any hint before last autumn that he was so inclined. Did that make him a hypocrite?

Never once, however, had he accepted the conclusion of others that he was a virtuous man or loudly shouted that he was not so others would praise him even more for his merits. Instead, he stood quietly in the background until needed, was remarkably humble, and always kind to those in need.

Surely that suggested he was no hypocrite. Perhaps his fight against this thorn in his flesh, as St Paul once called his own torment, would cleanse him in God's eyes. Hadn't that valiant fight worked for the saints she recalled?

His deep melancholy, hours spent in the chapel, and his visits to the anchoress suggested he was suffering profoundly. That was not the way of an evil man. Yet he had not sought confession, nor had he come to her to admit what had happened.

Why?

But something had clearly changed after he returned from talking to Master Durant and his wife in Norwich. Now he was planning to seek Brother John for confession and penance. He seemed to have found a purpose in the prospect of caring for the mutilated vintner. And the monk's eyes had brightened when she asked him to question the injured carpenter so the investigation could begin before Ralf was able to take over.

The cat awoke, scrubbed a paw, and went back to sleep.

I must be patient, Eleanor concluded. Now is not the time to make decisions. I must leave it to God to tell me what to do.

She steadfastly believed in God's mercy when repentance was sincere. Yes, she desperately wanted to keep her monk at her side, not because of lust, but out of a chaster love and need for his insights. As a pair, they served God well in bringing murderers to justice. Why would He cast that aside if Brother Thomas genuinely suffered and repented over whatever had happened?

For the first time, Eleanor began to feel hope again about Brother Thomas and to believe she could turn her mind to other problems. There was Gytha and her ill health. Surely the young woman would consult Sister Anne. If anyone had an answer that God would not abhor, it would be the sub-infirmarian. She smiled with relief.

"Very well," Eleanor said to the cat. "It is time I got back to accounts and you returned to Sister Matilda. She needs your sharp eyes and swift pursuit of rodents, O Master of Kitchens."

Arthur looked up at her and yawned, making sure all his sharp teeth were well displayed. He jumped from her lap, had a good stretch, and strode out the door.

Eleanor went back to the window and, with a happier spirit, looked out at the view.

Color had returned to the outside world.

CHAPTER ELEVEN

As Thomas walked past the chapel with its moss-covered windows, walls stained with black mildew and etched with the ravages of age, he decided to make one stop at the anchoress' window before going into the village and questioning the carpenter, Oswin. He needed the strength of her counsel.

He had long respected Anchoress Juliana and had been her confessor since her arrival ten years ago. Her initial struggles were legendary. Even today, she bore the scars on her head and face where she had hurled herself against the walls of her cell until her flesh wept blood.

The violence had not been committed because she hated her stern vocation, but because she felt unworthy of it. That much he knew as her confessor. Then, rather abruptly, she calmed and since had become known for her serenity and wisdom instead of her howls of spiritual pain.

Thomas wished his attempts at solace had been the reason for the change, but he doubted his words had helped. More likely, he concluded, God had come to her one night, while she lay sleepless in the grave she had dug for herself with her own broken nails, and taken her hand, giving her the comfort no man could. When asked for the cause of her current peace, her answer was invariably a gentle smile and silence.

But now it was she who offered him solace.

Although the Church demanded that women remain silent, having been created second but erring first, an anchoress had an unusual status founded in her harsher vocation. For mortal women, redemption from Eve's sin was usually found in the agony of childbirth. But the anchoress avoided even the plainest of earthly delights by enclosing herself behind walls after a ceremony that declared her dead. For this more rigorous virtue, God occasionally used her tongue to bring His teachings to men.

As Thomas turned toward Juliana's anchorage on the other side of the chapel, he saw a skeletally thin village woman kneeling at the curtained window. To allow her privacy for needed consolation, he stepped back behind some bushes and leaned against the wall of the building that remained cold even in summer.

"I have always found comfort in the company of women," he murmured. When he swore never again to lie with any woman, he had felt an odd relief but failed to understand why. Women also seemed to feel their bodies were safe with him and valued his unusual understanding of their sins.

I might own the shape of a man, he thought, but I sometimes fear I was given a woman's heart. Would that explain my own longing to bond with a man? Or am I simply a failed bit of creation that God accidentally gave the breath of life?

But God does not make mistakes, he reminded himself and then peeked through the shrubbery to see if the guest at the window was still there.

The woman was still there. It was someone he recognized. Had she been beaten by her husband again or was her heart bleeding over his latest public mockery of her? Whatever the woman's sorrows, Juliana would find words to give her the strength to endure and then voice them in a manner that suggested she understood more than she had been told—as she often did.

Thomas straightened and looked up at the faded blue sky above him.

He had never told the anchoress about his longing to lie with men but that hadn't mattered. When he went to her window, fighting tears and losing the battle, she had only spoken of prayer and God's mercy, but he had found the gift of peace in her tone. Especially after his return last autumn, the feeling that she understood his grief and did not curse him as Satan's creature was what kept him from committing self-murder.

He heard a sound and carefully peered again through the shrub. The woman was walking away. Thomas waited until she had disappeared before he approached the window.

§

He quietly knelt but did not need to speak. She always knew who it was.

"Brother Thomas, you are welcome." The anchoress' voice, deep and warm, soothed his hidden wounds like one of Sister Anne's ointments.

Thomas briefly recounted the vintner's tale, the sanctuary Durant had begged, and how he longed to give the man the care he had requested. "But I fear that I would corrupt him with my sins were I to do so," he said. "My wickedness is no less than that of Satan himself."

He heard a sharp intake of breath, but otherwise she did not respond for a long moment.

"Have you heard the tale of Robert the Devil, Brother?" Her tone was conversational, with no hint of disgust or condemnation.

"I have not."

"It is in a manuscript that has just been added to the priory library. I recommend that you read it. A short tale, but a comforting one to those of us who have committed grave offenses with our bodies or souls."

Knowing she would explain further, he silently waited.

"Robert was a man of great beauty and warrior skills, gifts that surpassed those granted most mortal men, but he was also wicked, cruel, and prone to attacks of unreasonable violence. One day, unable to bear the evil part of his nature, he went to his mother and begged her, if she knew, to tell him why he was this way. She finally explained that she had been barren and made a pact with the Devil so she might bear her husband the needed son and heir. Robert was the result, and, according to the agreement she had made, his soul belonged to the Prince of Darkness."

"How could any mother curse a child so cruelly through eternity?" Thomas went numb. Had his own mother done such a thing? Was this why he had been cursed with his forbidden longings? Yet he knew his mother had had no reason to want a son, or indeed any child. He was born a bastard, the spawn of a presumably brief union between servant and lord.

"But he was not so condemned, Brother. In his grief, he sought out the pope and a holy hermit." She started to say more, then stopped. "I shall not tell you how the tale ended. Read it for yourself, ponder, and seek out our own holy hermit, Brother John. It is he who must explain the meaning of the tale to you and answer your questions."

"I do not doubt God's mercy, but some evil ways are so dark that even God cannot forgive them. Satan uses sins like mine as fuel for Hell's fires."

"The timing of the arrival of this manuscript and the vintner's plea cannot be coincidence, Brother. I feel certain that you will agree that there is a similarity between your sorrows and those of Robert the Devil. You must seek Brother John without further delay and confess the sins you hate so much. I am sure our hermit is familiar with the tale I mentioned and will explain how it relates to your sins and order a proper penance."

"Why will you not tell me the rest of the story?"

"I am only a simple woman and cannot speak with a priest's authority. I also think you must read the story yourself so you can direct the right questions to Brother John. Do no forget that the path to salvation is different for each of us. God's grace is infinite for the heart that longs for His love." There was a brief silence, then she added in a soft whisper, "Robert the Devil was given mercy even though his soul had been granted to the Prince of Darkness."

Thomas felt as if a hand had just caressed the top of his head with a mother's tenderness, but knew it was more likely a breeze from the sea. Then a small voice from his soul hissed doubt that he had any reason for hope.

He willed it into silence.

Rising, he placed his hand on the ledge of the anchoress's window. "You have given me hope once again," he said. "I would bless you for it, but the gift of your wisdom is far too great for my imperfect words to thank."

"I am a daughter of Eve, Brother. If you have found hope in my mutterings, it is because God has used my lips to bring it to you."

As he left the anchoress' window for his task in the village, Thomas vowed to read the tale of Robert the Devil later in the day. Even if he must wait for the hermit's explanation of the story, he now knew how he might confess the depth of his sins to Brother John.

CHAPTER TWELVE

A man leaned back against the wall near a corner as he watched a monk enter the inn and stop to talk with the innkeeper's boy.

Lifting his jack of ale, he swallowed the bitter drink, put the jack down on the nearby table, and bent his head to trim a broken nail with his knife.

Now why would a tonsured man come to an inn?

Not that many of those vowed to God were as virtuous as they proclaimed themselves to be, but he was not inclined to believe all the jests. And this was the village next to Tyndal Priory, one belonging to the Order of Fontevraud and well known for pious works. It was also home to a holy anchoress, and a prioress who had been granted a vision of the Holy Family some years ago. Since this fellow, chatting to the brat, was dressed in a habit belonging to that religious order, it was more reasonable to conclude that he had come to cleanse some frightened soul in time to face God and not because he wanted to rent a plump whore.

He rubbed his chin and winced at the unaccustomed roughness. His stubbly beard had been left to grow for a reason, he reminded himself, and he would soon be able to shave it off.

He went back to pondering the meaning of the monk talking to the lad.

There was the man found beaten in the square last night. When discovered, he was barely alive. Some boy, likely returning from swyving his girl, had frightened the assailant before he had killed the man.

A villager had told him, over a companionable offer of ale, that the innkeeper put the victim in quarters outside the inn. But how long would a man so wounded be able to live? His hold on life must be weakening and that would certainly account for the monk's visit here. As for the lad he was talking to? He worked at the inn and would know where the dying man lay.

But why had the man been attacked so viciously?

Did he even care?

He began to smile as a thought occurred to him.

"You look oddly pensive."

A man had slid in next to him, but he hadn't noticed. He was startled but wise enough to hide his reaction. Calmly, he looked at the speaker and was relieved that he was no stranger.

He winked. "You would too if you had just seen a vision of an earthly angel," he replied. "Have you gazed upon the innkeeper? Her breasts alone would keep a man happy in bed any time of the year, let alone…" He licked his lips.

"I care not for any innkeeper's breasts," the man said, his voice sharp with irritation.

"I never imagined you were inclined to celibacy."

The man's face looked oddly pale in the dim light, and his one visible hand was clenched so tight the knuckles were white.

The man shoved the jug of ale closer to his visitor. "Never mind. Drink this. It is good. But what troubles you?"

"We must talk."

"Perhaps so." The desired discussion suited him. They both had something each wished to resolve. "Say more."

"Not here."

He shrugged and tried to hide his annoyance at yet another delay.

Sitting with nothing to do was beginning to eat at him. He had grown weary of this place, especially after he found that the innkeeper was not only a virtuous woman but expected her wenches to be as well.

"Tonight. Near the mill door entrance to the priory. When the inn closes its door, I shall travel there first. Follow soon after but do not take a light. The moon is full enough."

The man nodded. A night meeting without a torch did not seem wise to him, especially if there was a violent man in the village who wasn't just avenging some perceived assault on his wife's virtue.

But he was more accustomed to larger places than this village, where dangers were greater, and he had cause enough to talk with this fellow. Surely tiny Tyndal would be safe enough at night.

He would chance it.

CHAPTER THIRTEEN

Nute quickly looked around the inn and, failing to see Signy, told Brother Thomas he would be happy to answer any questions.

"You chased away the assailant after finding the wounded man last night." Thomas grinned. "Your foster mother must be proud to have brought up such a brave son."

Nute blushed. "I failed, Brother, and have nothing to boast about."

"How so?"

"I should have caught the culprit. Instead, I let him escape."

"Catching him was not required, lad. In getting help for the wounded man, you saved his life."

Nute shook his head. "It was my duty to capture the attacker. Before Crowner Ralf left for the coast, he said I should watch the village at night. With so many strangers stopping here on their journey home from visiting St. Walstan's shrine, there might well be miscreants, hiding in the pilgrim bands, who wished to take advantage of the unwary and even our villagers."

Thomas wondered about this task allegedly assigned to Nute by the crowner. It did not seem a responsibility appropriate to Nute's age and lack of experience. Ralf was fond of the lad. Why charge him with an undertaking that could prove dangerous?

Taking care not to sound dismissive, Thomas asked, "Did he actually say you should do this or did you take on the responsibility out of love for our crowner?"

When Nute quickly looked away, Thomas had his answer. Ralf might well have praised the concept of a night watchman as a clever one in principle but would be horrified when he learned that Nute had picked up a cudgel and become the sole guardian of Tyndal village.

When Nute looked back, his face was still pink but his mind had regained focus on the events of last night. "But only I had the opportunity to catch him, Brother! Once I did so, I could have called for help in locking him up until our crowner returned."

Thomas decided not to pursue his question about what Ralf had actually agreed to with the youth. It was the crowner's task to balance praise for Nute's courage with a good scolding for taking unacceptable risks.

"Given two hard choices, I think you picked the best," Thomas said. "Had you chased after the man, the victim might have died of his wounds with the delay in getting help from our hospital." He shook his head. "And the attacker may well have made his escape into the night beyond hope of capture."

Nute thought about this, then reluctantly nodded.

"But you are a crucial witness. What did you see?"

"Little enough, Brother. I heard a shout, then a scream, so ran to the square from whence I thought the commotion was coming. The moonlight was only bright enough to see a body on the ground and a man running away." He closed his eyes as if reimagining the events. "It wouldn't have been bright enough for me to see many details. I think the assailant raised a hand, and he may have held a weapon. He did not appear to be unusually tall or short, but I could not guess his age. He did flee swiftly, which suggests he was young enough to run well." He shrugged. "I only saw the back of his head. He never turned to look in my direction—unless he did so from the shadows."

Thomas patted the youth's shoulder in approval. Nute had always been a patient and clever observer even as a child. When Thomas had lived briefly in the hermitage, now inhabited by Brother John, Nute hid in the shrubbery nearby to make sure the food he brought from Signy was not stolen by some wild creature or a passing traveler before Thomas retrieved it. Although he did finally notice the concealed child, it had taken him a while to do so.

"Anything else, now that you have had time to think more on it? An odd smell, perhaps? Was anything dropped at the site?"

"No, Brother. Only the smell of sweat but nothing to suggest the type of labor that might have caused it."

Once again, Thomas was impressed with Nute's observational ability. A fisherman would stink of fish, a butcher of blood, and a blacksmith of smoke.

Nute had paused to think. "As for anything dropped, I found nothing, and I did check the ground after the sun rose enough to see clearly. I doubt anyone would have stolen something left. The men who gathered in the square after the attack were either eager to help or only interested in a tale to tell their wives."

"Do you know of any reason why the carpenter was attacked? And what do you know of him?"

The youth took time in answering. "We know little enough about him. His name is Oswin. He claims to come from Norwich, and his accent supports his story. Some time ago, he heard that he could earn more working on ship repairs so left to seek employment on the coast. When he chose to return home, he was attacked by outlaws on the road and lost all he had acquired. He was unable to safely travel the short distance to Norwich and had nothing to bring his family. Thus he stopped here to earn it. My foster mother needed work done on our house, and our village lacked a carpenter after the last one died. Oswin seemed honest, and she hired him."

Thomas knew that Signy was rarely wrong in her assessment of others. Not only was she revered in the village for her charity and virtue, despite an almost celestial beauty, she was known for her skills in reading men's souls. "Has he done good work for her?"

"Aye, Brother. He does not mingle much with the villagers,

although he is courteous enough, and he sleeps in the stable hay where he also eats the meals the kitchen gives him."

"So he has not found companionship with any man or even a woman?"

Nute shook his head.

But the monk sensed that he was holding something back. "What did you think of him? He was working on the house where you lived. You must have had conversation."

The lad frowned. "He seemed kind enough. When we passed by each other, he smiled and wished me God's mercy for the day." Looking around, Nute lowered his voice. "Just the other day, he offered to help me with an excuse for my foster mother."

Thomas realized the lad did not want to be overheard and moved closer.

"She does not approve of my work for our crowner, and I over-slept once when I should have been at the inn to help her. Oswin offered to come with me and tell her that I was helping him, as an excuse for my delay. But when we arrived at the door, he suddenly stopped and said I should tell her myself that I was helping him with a repair. He did say he would confirm it if she asked."

"And did he?"

"My mother did not think my failure to help her was so easily excusable."

Puzzled, Thomas asked, "What made him change his mind?"

"I cannot be sure, Brother, but his face was pale, and he clearly did not want to go any further into the inn. My suspicion was that he may have seen someone but did not want to be seen himself." He bit his lip. "You asked if there was any reason for the attack. Before that incident, I would have said I knew of none. After, I wonder if there was."

"Did you think him an honest man?" The lad might be young but he had good wits and an older man's more knowledgeable sensitivity about character.

"There is something about Oswin that troubles me, Brother. I confess that I do not quite trust him, yet I also believe him to be a kind man."

CHAPTER FOURTEEN

When Brother Thomas entered the hut, a lean woman of indeterminate years looked over her shoulder. She saw who the visitor was, greeted him with a smile, and stepped back from her patient.

The carpenter lay motionless in his bed and gazed with half-opened eyes at Thomas. Weariness was the only expression on his gray face.

Thomas returned the nurse's smile. "I regret this intrusion, Mistress Hilde, but I must speak with Oswin alone."

Nodding, she swiftly made sure that nothing was immediately required for her patient. "If you require anything, Brother, I will be helping the cook in the kitchen." Then she vanished so quickly one might doubt she had ever been there.

The man in the bed did not move or even beg a blessing, as was common for most in his weakened condition.

Thomas took a moment to study Oswin. There was no suggestion of defiance in his eyes, he thought, yet resignation oozed like sweat from the wounded man. Those injuries were painful, but the carpenter knew he was likely to live. He should have shown some happiness, yet he looked as if grimly resolved to a harder fate.

Thomas now understood why Nute felt uneasy about the carpenter. His reactions suggested something unknown was causing this melancholia. What was it? Was it important to know why, either because of the attack on him or anything else the crowner might find interesting? Or was it a profound personal sorrow that meant nothing except to Oswin?

"I am Brother Thomas from Tyndal Priory. May we provide anything from the hospital or priory for your comfort? Greater relief for pain? Someone to pray with you?"

The carpenter smiled. "A lay brother frequently comes to examine my wounds, and Mistress Signy has provided more comfort than I imagined existed. The widow who attends me is both diligent and kind."

Thomas noted that the carpenter did not mention the need for confession or prayer, but he also saw why Nute liked this man. His manner of speech was warm, with no hint of dissembling. His tone matched his words in appreciation for the care given. Yet

Thomas remained convinced that Oswin was not without secrets and was beginning to suspect that they were greater than the common sins of the average man.

"Have you strength enough to answer a few queries? Crowner Ralf is far from here, and his return will be delayed, but my prioress has offered to gather all possible information about the attack on you. She will, of course, relay all to him when he comes back. It is important to do so when the details are still vivid to all."

A frown briefly appeared in the carpenter's forehead and just as quickly vanished. "I have heard of Prioress Eleanor's reputation as well as yours, Brother. I need no explanation for your visit on the crowner's behalf. Ask what you will, and I shall answer as I can."

Catching a subtle change of expression on the man's face, Thomas wondered if he was relieved that the crowner hadn't come. It was a thought he would hold on to until proven wrong. "Then I must first ask why you were out so late last night?"

"I could not sleep. The air was warm. Being past first youth, my body occasionally suffers from the day's labor. I hoped I would be able to sleep if I went into the village, where the sea breeze might cool me and banish the aches."

"Did you see anyone else?"

"Nothing human or devilish." Again, he briefly smiled. "Unless you think cats belong to Satan's choir. Two males were fighting over a female. Apparently enamored of neither, she yawned and left. When they realized she had gone, they stopped hissing and departed as well —in separate directions."

Thomas laughed.

Suddenly, Oswin winced, and the color the sun had given his face turned white. But he waved away Thomas's concern and asked for the next question.

"I shall not tire you much further, but I must know if you have offended anyone in the village for any reason since you arrived."

"I did not steal the chance for labor from any villager. The carpenter here had died, and there was no one to replace him. Since I need to save all coin Mistress Signy gives me for my labor, I do not spend on drink, nor do I take up room in her inn. The cook gives me my meals and a jack of ale, which I take to my bed in the stable straw. I do not see how I could have offended any man. I do not mingle with the villagers, yet I speak with courtesy to all who choose to greet me. I am a stranger here, and all understand that I will leave when I can." He hesitated. "Yet I find the inhabitants of the village surprisingly welcoming. Nay, I know of no ill will."

Thomas realized the effort to say that much had taken most of the man's strength. "One last question?"

"Aye, Brother." It was clear that Oswin strained to even whisper.

"What do you remember of the attack or the one who beat you?"

"Nothing."

The one word reply was understandable. The carpenter had little strength left, but there was something in the man's tone that troubled him. Had Oswin answered too quickly? If he had more information, he should have asked if Thomas could return later when he was rested. Or was there a little shifting of his eyes that hinted he did not intend to say anything more no matter what he recalled?

Once again, Thomas agreed with Nute. However pleasant the carpenter seemed, there was something in his demeanor that suggested he was not quite trustworthy.

Thomas nodded. "I shall leave you for now."

Oswin's eyes had dulled with gray fatigue, tinted only with that darker hue of unexplained resignation.

"I may have to return," Thomas said, "but will not trouble you otherwise. Should you remember anything at all, please send for me unless the crowner has come back. In the meantime, our priory will continue to do all we can to heal you. Shall I send for Mistress Hilde?"

Oswin nodded and flashed a weary smile, but he still had not asked for a blessing.

Thomas left for the kitchen to fetch Mistress Hilde himself.

CHAPTER FIFTEEN

As Nute dutifully performed his required tasks at the inn, he pondered, grumbled, and felt guilty in equal proportions.

Like everyone else in the village, he admired his mother's charity to those in need. On many occasions, he delivered food or coin to doors, knocked, and fled so the person would not know from whom the gift had come. They all did, of course. But when the innkeeper was confronted and thanked, her inevitable response was that if God cared about sparrows, why would He not also provide for the creatures He had made in His own image? That she was the village saint he never questioned. He was proud of her.

Although she had no obligation to have done so, she embraced him and Ingerith with a mother's love and determined protection after their parents died of a sweating sickness. Nute was fully aware that the love she bore them was not founded in duty. Both he and his sister returned it unreservedly.

What he did not like was her current and increasingly frequent rough greeting to him when he arrived at the inn. There were few men, in full armor or not, who could terrify as much as Signy did when outraged. She never raised her voice. She had no need. Her words were like dagger points and could slash like a whip.

When he saw the storm clouds gathering in her eyes, darkening their blue color into a more ominous shade, he wondered if God might not be more of a Mother than a Father. Even the man he loved, and who had taken on the role of his father, Crowner Ralf, trembled when she had a quarrel with him.

He did not understand why she objected to his wish to join the crowner's men. He did not have his sister's interest in all aspects of running an inn. Food to him was something you ate to stop your stomach from growling. As long as it wasn't rotten, he didn't care what it tasted like. Ingerith, on the other hand, spent hours with the cook discussing seasoning herbs and even visited Sister Matilda at the priory for ideas. Young though she was, his sister had actually persuaded their foster mother to incorporate ideas for simple but appealing dishes at reasonable cost.

But Nute needed action to be content. Maybe his mother couldn't understand because she was a woman. Women didn't seem to grasp the joy in overpowering a brigand, wrestling him to the ground, and dragging him off to face the consequences of his crimes before the king's justice.

He stopped sweeping for a moment. Well, perhaps Prioress Eleanor might, he thought, but she was working on God's behalf, which put her efforts on a spiritual level. He was content to deal with more common crimes than those that warranted God's attention.

Putting the broom aside and taking a rag to wipe up spills on tables, he admitted to himself that more thrilled him than a simple capture of some miscreant. It was also the challenge of figuring out who the person was, then outwitting him, which delighted. That part was something he thought his mother should understand. Many said that women weren't rational, but few could match her wits and perception. Maybe that was because she was a saint, but Nute also had to admit that his sister was pretty clever herself, and he saw no hints of sainthood in her twinkling eyes.

The wood was chopped in the proper sizes for roasting meat and cooking stews. He piled it close to the kitchen so the cook would not have to carry it far. Brushing off his hands, he went into the inn and began to clear off bowls and jacks to save the serving women time. Then he looked around to see if anything else needed attention so he would not have to seek out the innkeeper for instruction. While they were having this difficult time, he wished no more contact with her than was obligatory.

Suddenly, he saw how he could serve both his mother's wishes and his own at the same time. While he visited with the inn customers and helped the serving women, he could hone his skills at observation, something both Crowner Ralf and Brother Thomas had told him was crucial in the hunting of outlaws. With the inn still busy with strangers coming from St. Walstan's shrine, he had much opportunity to notice details of behavior and then ponder what they might mean.

In the far corner, for instance, he saw three men bending toward each other in close conversation. Did that not suggest that the topic under discussion was very important to them all? And might it be something they did not want any stranger close to them to overhear?

Nute reached for a pitcher of ale and edged toward the interesting trio. As he approached, chatting and serving others, he kept his expression casual and carefully betrayed no interest in his quarry in the corner.

What first caught his attention, out of the corner of his eye, was the disparate attire of the men.

The one nearest him was dressed in a robe of rough cloth, perhaps hemp. The one in the middle was dressed simply, as a pilgrim ought, but the cloth looked like a summer-weight linen and was suggestive of a man with greater means. The third man's attire was less indicative of rank. In part, his clothes looked like he might have worked in the fields, sweat-stained and mended, yet his boots were sturdy. Might he be an overseer of laborers? All had beards of varying lengths, so Nute could not see expressions or faces clearly, and he was too far away to read their eyes.

He inched closer.

Now he could hear their voices, though not enough to tell what they were discussing.

The first man might be a servant, Nute decided. He said little and bent forward, not like an equal participant in the discussion, but as if he needed to know what the other two might want him to do.

The more affluent man was likely a merchant, Nute now decided, his speech a mixed dialect from a rural youth and a long residency as a man in Norwich. His intense expression and controlled gestures suggested he was trying hard to persuade the third man of something.

The third man with the well-made boots now sat back and twisted his jack of ale around on the table. For a man likely to be a laborer or farm overseer at best, he seemed oddly lacking in deference to the speaker, who must be of higher status.

Nute was confused. Taking the presumed servant out of the trio, what could two such different men have in common? Even if they had joined in the pilgrimage together, their current behavior toward each other seemed inexplicable. It was unlikely that they were arguing a point of faith. That was for clerics, not worldly men. What could they be discussing that would allow such familiarity? Might they be related? Was the third man a friend from the merchant's youth? Or...

In his eagerness to learn more, Nute made a mistake.

The third man caught him staring and gestured to his companions. All conversation ceased. The merchant folded his arms and studied the straw under his feet.

"Another pitcher of ale?" Nute asked brightly. "A bowl of our thick pottage, made with vegetables fresh from our own garden and seasoned with the cook's secret herbs?"

Silently, he cursed himself for his lack of subtlety.

They waved him away.

As he left to serve others, Nute knew he had learned an important lesson, then chose another group of customers to observe.

He would practice greater cunning with them.

CHAPTER SIXTEEN

Signy watched Gytha slowly lift the wooden spoon full of pigeon stew with vegetables, then sip. To the innkeeper's mind, the smell of sweet young onions, earthy mushrooms, fruity purple carrots, and pungent green herbs would not only wake the dead, but bring a pleasant smile to their faces. She could only hope it would sharpen her friend's appetite.

Gytha put her spoon down.

"Eat," Signy said, trying not to treat the crowner's wife as she would her foster daughter. She knew from Gytha's amused expression that she had failed.

"Another spoonful? I know those words well, although there is less of a need with sons than with our daughter."

Signy loved that Gytha considered Ralf's daughter hers as well, but that thought did not make her forget her purpose here. "And one more bite after that," she said and deliberately frowned as a mother might. Then she burst into laughter and squeezed her friend's hand.

Gytha dutifully tore off a tiny piece of the loaf and ate it with determination. "I fear your cook's barley bread must be my last bite."

Signy sat back and sighed. "You are thin and pale. Not eating is dangerous, dear heart. You need strength. You have young children to care for, as well as a husband who adores you, and friends who need you."

"I know," Gytha replied and struggled to eat a little more of the now cooling stew. Finally, she put the spoon down and closed her eyes. She made no effort to disguise that exhaustion easily vanquished her.

"You have not recovered from your miscarriage," Signy said, pushing her own bowl aside, knowing that she must speak bluntly to her friend. The women usually met once a week in this quiet of Signy's house, where they could gossip and confide in each other away from business and family demands. If she was going to help resolve what was troubling the crowner's wife, it had to be now.

"I will not pretend I have, and my poor health is affecting my family."

"You must see Sister Anne. You will not be the first woman who has struggled after so many births, and you have already given your husband a fine family."

Gytha began to cry.

Signy immediately rose and went to hold her. "What is it? There is nothing you cannot tell me." Yet she dreaded what she might learn. Life was a fragile gift in the best of times. Just how ill was her friend?

Her tears subsiding, Gytha dried her cheeks. "My fear is not just about the effect on our babes. It is Ralf as well."

Signy felt her face turn hot. "I will geld the man if he has hurt you!"

She had reason for her anger. Years before his marriage to Gytha, Ralf had taken Signy to bed, then called out another woman's name while he swyved her. She had loved him, and her heart was crushed when she knew he had used her body because he couldn't lie with another. In time, they had made peace, but the wound had never fully healed. If he ever hurt this good wife of his, Signy believed she might actually kill him.

"He has not, Signy! The fear is one we share. After this miscarriage and my failure to recover, we cannot lie together. God has given me great fertility, and I quicken as soon as I can after the last babe. Until now, I have remained strong, but this miscarriage…"

Signy nodded.

"Ralf says he is terrified the next pregnancy will kill me. I look at my babes and beg God not to take my soul until they are old enough to have their own families. Maybe that is selfish of me. If God wills it otherwise…" Another tear rolled down her cheek.

"Death may be common, but surely God understands a mother's longing to care for the little ones who still need her. He cannot believe that is a selfish wish."

"I do not remember my own mother or father, but my brother does. He became both parents to me." She tried to smile. "Even as a young lad, he was gentle, yet few in the village were as strong. No one quarreled with him. Yet the responsibility of caring for a little girl must have been hard. He has never married and has no children of his own."

"Tostig is a good man." Signy rose, removed the bowls of congealed stew, and poured them each a mazer of ale. Sitting down, she sipped the drink and returned to the discussion. "You say that Ralf will not lie with you now?"

"We both fear it so much that even the chastest of gestures are abandoned lest they lead to coupling. We no longer hug each other or touch hands!" She put her hands over her face and groaned. "Neither of us can bear this. It is torture."

"This cannot continue, Gytha. The Church allows husband and wife to enjoy the pleasures of the marriage bed unless both choose abstinence." Signy understood the problem very well. She may have rejected both marriage and taking a lover, but she had lost her virginity long ago and was hardly ignorant of the comforts of passion.

"We would not have married if we were capable of abstinence."

Signy waited for Gytha to finish all she needed to say.

"It is not just the physical pleasure in coupling, Signy; we feel more complete and also stronger in faith and our ability to perform worldly duties afterward." She blushed. "I wish I could explain it well. It feels like we have become Adam and Eve in the Garden. Our coupling is akin to becoming one again. I return the gift of his rib, and he receives it with love." She turned her face away. "Forgive me, but I cannot explain it better than that."

"You express it well," Signy said with gentleness. Despite her quarrels with Ralf and her momentary fury just now, she knew he adored his wife. Although she was incapable of such a thing herself, she knew that theirs was a truly happy marriage, and she found joy in that. That kind of marriage was a rare gift and not something she wanted to see crumble.

"I insist you go immediately to Sister Anne. You need advice, not only on regaining your health but on how to preserve it. That will do much to bring back everything else you and Ralf long to recover."

Gytha blinked as she suddenly realized what Signy meant with her careful phrasing. "We do not resent bringing more souls into the world for God..."

"I did not think you did. You simply need time between each new soul."

"That is a sin!"

"Is self-murder not a sin as well? I have never discussed this with a priest. But might conceiving, when you are so weakened that you might die of the birthing, be a form of self-murder?"

"I do not understand."

Signy shrugged. "I am not the one to advise on the what is or is not sin, dear heart. Speak with Sister Anne."

"A nun would never advise me on a way to prevent quickening. Perhaps I should talk to Brother Thomas and confess..."

"A good man indeed, one we all revere for his quiet goodness, but go first to our sub-infirmarian. She will not condemn you for honesty. Her father was a doctor, one who was renowned for his compassion as well as his skills. She learned from him and was an apothecary before she took vows. She must have treated other women who suffered ill health after a birth. All you need do is seek her advice on your health. You should also explain what damage this has caused in your marriage. If anyone does, she will be the most likely to have a remedy that is not sinful. That is why I recommend seeking her counsel and not that of a midwife." Signy took another drink of ale.

"Regaining your health is too important, Gytha. Your babes are so young."

Her friend nodded. "Sibley has grown somber too and no longer smiles. I think she fears she will lose me as she did her true mother."

"You have become her true mother."

"I love her as if that were so."

"Then promise me that you will consult Sister Anne without delay."

"I give you my word." Gytha looked around and saw that the cold pottage was gone. "I have wasted good food," she said sadly.

"Pottage is better a second day," Signy said. "I will give it to my Nute, unworthy lad that he is. When your Fulke reaches that age, I warn you that your garden must be doubled. He will eat the very foundation of your manor if he doesn't get enough in his stomach. Lads are ravenous."

The two women laughed, and Gytha ate another bite of bread.

CHAPTER SEVENTEEN

The worst of Oswin's pain did not come from his ribs, but from his soul.

Had the hospital lay brother not insisted that he must lie in bed to rest, he would have returned to his assigned place in the stable loft. Although the widow charged with his care was kind, he balked at her compassion. He needed to burn with anger, not indulge in the softness of comfort, and for rage he needed to be alone. He had a murder to plan.

Gentleness was a concept in which he no longer had faith. He could not even imagine it without mocking laughter. His soul had fallen into a black hole, pulsing with hate and the aching need for revenge. It was that need that seared him with hellish fire and stabbed at him with unrelenting agony, not a cracked rib, a little fever, or a dented skull.

And thus he had lied to the red-haired monk. He even lied to the widow whose soft eyes made him wish he were not a demon, but a man again. He still remembered when he had known how to love his friends and once had a family that had brought him joy. But that life had been torn away, and the only thing left to him was the need to kill.

So he snarled at the poor woman as if he hated the very sight of her and resented every bit of thoughtfulness. His hatred needed feeding. But he also knew he was cruel to use Mistress Hilde for that, and thus, occasionally, he remembered to smile and even thank her.

Of course he knew the man who had attacked him. He had seen his face after the first blow and before he lost consciousness. It was not one he would likely forget—nor the person to whom his assailant was bound.

Despite the passing years and the long beard and hair Oswin had grown, he now knew he had been recognized. In a way, he wished young Nute had not rescued him before he had been beaten to death. If he had died that night, the only sin left on his soul would be hate and murderous intent. That was likely the difference between a long suffering in Purgatory and eternity in Hell.

Yet he had fully understood that he would spend forever in hellfire when he came back to England. Why wish now that he could have avoided his purpose?

Oswin tried to turn over, but this time his ribs did hurt and he groaned. If he was so weak that this minor pain caused him to cry out like a babe, how much worse was the agony of Hell? He snorted in contempt at his cowardly fears and quivering flesh. He knew that he must face the hangman and that he could never repent breaking the commandment against murder this one time.

A brief knock at the door kept his tears of self-pity from flooding down his cheeks.

He barked an order to enter.

Mistress Hilde came in, holding a tray. Quickly, she looked around the room to see if anything needed her attention.

Oswin's soul ached for her goodness and longed to shout that she must flee before he infected her with his wickedness.

She might be plain and of middle years, much as he, but her eyes missed little. Her charm was her gaze. Once, he had complained about something, and she had retorted with a raised eyebrow and a gentle tease. His instant reaction was to take offense until he saw the sparkle in her eyes and knew she had only meant to lighten his cares.

It was the one time he had laughed. It was the last time he had felt any humanity.

"I have brought your supper. It is best eaten hot." As if wary, she stood some distance from him, yet her voice remained kind.

"I have no wish for food," he snapped.

She put down the tray on the chest near the bed. "You are pale. In pain, methinks."

"And wouldn't you be if you had just been beaten and kicked!" He waved his fist at the tray. "Take that away. It does not please me to eat."

"And so you said when I brought sustenance this morning to break your fast." She tilted her head at the empty jack and bowl dropped carelessly on the floor near his bed. "Yet you have finished the meal despite your denials, with which your empty stomach did not agree. And you have managed to fill the chamber pot well enough." She pointed to the odiferous object under discussion.

He knew he was flushing. "I changed my mind," he mumbled. Not since his dead wife had a woman spoken to him this way. Something akin to embarrassment mixed with regret stirred inside him. This emotion was not something he wanted to feel. It did nothing to keep his mind focused on his lethal purpose.

The widow picked up the chamber pot, left, and soon returned with it empty and cleaned. She put it by his bedside and stared down at him, one hand on her hip.

He tried to scowl and failed. Her look held no malice, only a quiet curiosity, as if she were trying to read his soul. He looked away. "I confess to pain. I want to be left alone," he muttered, not because he really did, but because he wanted her to leave for her own good.

"I shall bring you the poppy juice that the lay brother left," she replied and turned to the table where a dose sat in a mazer. "Although..."

"Leave it here, mistress," he said in a calm tone. He pointed to the floor next to his hand. That was the side away from the injured ribs and one he could reach.

"The lay brother said—"

"I will take more of it when I want to sleep." His tone was hard. "Perhaps I shall want to eat later," he said, this time trying to soften his tone. "Leave the food."

"The poppy juice in the mazer was all the lay brother left for a last dose of the day." She waited to see his response. "I must tell him if you need more than he had allowed."

He suddenly understood that she feared he might wish to commit self-murder by taking more than the permitted amount. It was no secret that poppy juice not only dulled pain, but also banished a life of suffering if too much was drunk. "And that mazer is all I shall require to sleep, mistress. I doubt you need to beg more from the lay brother, and I shall not summon you to bring me more in the middle of the night." He knew she slept just outside the door in case he cried out, but he also knew she slept deeply and was not easily awakened unless she sensed something amiss.

He hoped to take advantage of that.

All she did was nod, tidy a few items, place the draught where he had indicated, and pick up the morning dishes. "Is there anything you desire before I return?"

"Nothing until morning," he replied.

With a brief but sad look, she left.

But her last glance troubled him. Did she suspect what he meant to do?

CHAPTER EIGHTEEN

It is our nature to fear the night. Even when the stars remind us that angels do hover over the earth and God crafted the moon so a little light might chase away the occasional shadow, battle-hardened men still peer into the darkness for lurking demons and other imp-kissed creatures inclined to evil. Blood is most often shed out of rage, fear, or grief in the somber gloom of Satan's hours. It is not only dogs who howl at the moon.

In the village of Tyndal, few crimes occurred between those who were longtime neighbors and friends, but the population had been growing in recent years. As the priory hospital's reputation grew, and more came with their ailments and families, younger sons of distant merchants and craftsmen found profitable livelihoods settling there. Horses needed shoes. Carts broke down. Even gloves were lost.

So many strangers unsettled the older residents, and some grew wary of venturing out at night unless the need was vital. When the east brightened, however, fear vanished and everyone rose from their beds to break their fasts and begin their daily labors. God's sunlight meant the worst wickedness might be an argument, either soon ended or broken up.

So this man believed on his way with bags of grain on his cart to the mill built by the priory. When he saw a man lying on the ground near the mill gate, he assumed it was someone who had passed out last night from too much ale. He smiled, remembering his own evenings of too much drink before he married his lass.

When he approached to find out if the man needed help, a numbing chill of terror froze him in mid-step.

The unblinking eyes, wide-open mouth, and bloody gap in the neck belonged to a corpse.

Abandoning his cart, the man fled back to the village. Seeing Nute, he begged him to bring his club and come back to provide witness to the horrible crime.

*

Prioress Eleanor was just returning from prayer when Gracia stopped her and said that Nute was waiting in the audience chamber.

"He is quite pale," the young woman whispered to her prioress. Anticipating the first question, she added, "He did not say why he had come, only that his need to speak with you was urgent."

With Gracia following just behind, Eleanor entered her audience chamber.

Nute fell to his knees.

"Rise! I do not merit that reverence."

He staggered to his feet. "My lady, I must beg a favor from you. I do not know what else to do or where to go. A body has been found near the priory mill gate. Crowner Ralf is somewhere on the coast." He stretched his hands out to beseech her. "Will you help us?"

"Tell me all you can," she replied.

Without being asked, Gracia offered a mazer of ale to the lad, then went to stand by the door.

"A man found the corpse this morning on his way to the mill and ran back to the village for help. He saw me first, and we returned to where the man lay. I can confirm the man is dead." A sheen of sweat broke out on his forehead. "Even I knew it would not take Brother Thomas to conclude the man was murdered."

"Has the body been moved?"

"No, nor did the man touch the body before he sought help. He was reluctant to do so, but I begged him to guard the corpse until I return or someone comes from the priory." He bowed his head. "I hope you will forgive me for saying that. I had no right, but..."

Eleanor assured him that he had done well, then asked, "Could you identify the corpse, or is he a stranger?"

"A stranger, my lady, but I recognized him from the inn. I think he is one of the many who have been on pilgrimage to Bawburgh." He hesitated, closed his eyes, and swallowed several times to keep from vomiting.

Gracia hurried over and pushed a piece of bread into his hand. "Eat," she murmured. "It settles the stomach."

He flashed her a weak but grateful smile. "I do not know his name or where he comes from," he replied. "My foster mother might know more. I do not recall any quarrels he had with anyone. Pilgrims tend to come back from shrines far calmer than most men, and they drink less. That is why I thought it so odd that Oswin was attacked and why this murder is especially shocking."

An interesting observation, Eleanor thought. Nute was a bright lad. She shared the fondness for him felt by both Crowner Ralf and Brother Thomas.

"As you know, I have no authority outside this priory when a crime committed under the king's law takes place," she said, but her tone suggested a willingness to help.

Nute brightened.

"But with the crowner gone and this the second violent act in two days..."

"The villagers will be frightened, my lady. Our peace is shattered. There is now fatal bloodshed, and no perpetrator is known."

"I shall summon Brother Thomas and a few lay brothers. You can take him to examine the body, and the lay brothers will carry the corpse to our chapel. The dead body should lie under God's eye and not those of curious men."

Nute looked like he was about ready to weep with relief.

83

"But a messenger must be sent to the crowner to tell him about this crime as well as the beating of the carpenter. I can only do so much and dare not tread further on the legal rights of King Edward."

"I would go myself this instant to bring the crowner home, my lady, but my foster mother would forbid it."

Nute looked desperately eager to be that messenger, but Eleanor remembered what Gytha had told her about the recent difficulties between the lad and Signy. "I know you are needed at the inn," she replied. "Brother Thomas will be responsible for finding a way to get word to our crowner. I would be grateful if you told your mother that our monk may need her help. You have done well to bring this murder to our attention. I shall make sure she knows how grateful I am for that."

Nute struggled with himself, then clenched his fists. "Indeed, I must return to the inn as soon as possible, my lady. I am already late in helping my foster mother with tasks that must be done before she even opens the doors."

Eleanor glanced at Gracia, who raced from the room, leaving the door to the audience chamber open. Another young nun, who sometimes helped Eleanor with her accounting rolls, slipped in to take her place.

"You will not be long delayed, Nute. Brother Thomas will be here in a few moments. You can take him and the lay brothers to the body on your way back. Tell Signy that I grieve that I have kept you from your work. But I am also grateful it was you the man found to report the crime. You have been very helpful."

He blushed with pleasure, then swallowed the entire mazer of ale that Gracia had poured and grinned.

CHAPTER NINETEEN

Brother Thomas needed only a glance at the cut throat to conclude that the death was a murder and not the act of a despairing soul. No man could slash his own neck in that way, nor was it likely to occur by accident.

A few villagers had gathered, and Thomas knew he would be wise to complete what he needed to do immediately and move the body to the priory. The less time he spent—and the fewer curious men nearby to see details of the body—the less quickly rumor and attendant panic would spread.

He gestured for the lay brothers to approach. As they formed a small circle around him to allow some privacy, Thomas knelt. He quickly inspected the immediate area for evidence that might be lost when the corpse was moved. Then he began a superficial examination of the corpse to get immediate impressions that would produce questions for later resolution.

The dead man wore a simple robe, proper for one on pilgrimage, although the quality of cloth suggested he was not poor. Feeling the man's hands for calluses, he concluded that the man had not recently done hard labor. He also found no scars or immediate evidence of broken bones on them. It was probable that he was a merchant rather than a craftsman who might cut himself or crack a bone.

Might he be of Norman birth? A man of some little rank or even the progeny of a third or fourth son? The king and the law cared about that, even generations after the Battle of Hastings.

But excess sons took vows, jousted for rewards and glory, sought positions in the king's court, or sold themselves as leaders of mercenaries. And finally, why would a man of that heritage go on pilgrimage to honor the patron saint of farmers?

The dead man did suffer from swollen joints and slightly crooked fingers. That suggested a man of middle years, when the joint disease often began to torment mortals. The man's hair was mostly brown with only a little gray present. His beard was short and patchy. Thomas suspected the man had let it grow for the pilgrimage, but otherwise was probably clean-shaven.

Thomas tried to see the man's face where the facial hair did not disguise it. The nose was bulbous, the skin fair and slightly pitted, the bulging eyes hazel, and the ears were large. Sitting back, he noted that the man was short of stature but stocky. Nothing more about him suggested anything that would make identification possible.

But something troubled him. The man looked vaguely familiar. With so many pilgrims traveling through the village of late, it was probable he had seen the man on one of those days when he took medicines to those who were too aged or ill to go to the hospital. But why would he have noticed him? There was nothing striking about him.

"Brother?"

Startled, Thomas jumped to his feet and quickly hid his discomfort with a smile.

A man stood just behind one of the lay brothers, who had raised an arm to keep him from moving closer. "I do not wish to disturb you, Brother, but I might have information about this man. Were the crowner here, I would have told him."

"As he is not near the village, you may reveal what you need to me. When Crowner Ralf returns, I shall make sure he learns of it."

"I overheard a youth telling the innkeeper that a man in pilgrim's robes had been found dead down the road from the village. I decided to see if I could identify him since I have been staying at the inn."

Thomas stared at the speaker. "You, however, are not a pilgrim?"

"In my travels on behalf of my master, I arrived in Bawburgh at the time of the feast. I did honor the saint, as faith demanded, and then journeyed on with a large number of pilgrims for safety's sake. A few I spent time with in pleasant conversation, but those have already left for their homes, or so I thought." He nodded at the body. "Perhaps this was one who never made it that far?"

Thomas nodded to the lay brother, who stepped back to allow the speaker to approach the corpse.

The man knelt and looked closely at the dead man's face for a moment, then quickly rose. "I did share a table with him and others at the inn and remember he was in a party of those returning from the feast." He rose and shook his head. "A somber fellow. I doubt any of us exchanged more than a few words with him. He kept to himself. So I do not know his name, his home, or his profession, although I assumed he was a merchant from his dress and the closeness with which he kept his coin." He grinned. "He did not even buy a pitcher of ale for the table."

"No servant? No friends with whom he traveled?"

"A servant perhaps, one who sat next to him with head bowed toward his one jack of ale and said nothing. But I only assumed that relationship because I thought him rather cringing. Otherwise, this man seemed to be alone."

And all that is little help, Thomas thought. He wondered if anyone else at the inn might remember more. He frowned. If the dead man was a merchant—and the finer cloth of his robe suggested he had achieved some success in his work—then it was unlikely that he would have traveled without a servant. Was the servant still at the inn?

"I am surprised to see you outside your walls, Brother." The man raised his hands to suggest he meant no ill. "I expected the innkeeper to take the dead man to your priory, where his body could rest in the chapel until the crowner arrived. But to see a monk kneeling on this road and not at prayer..."

"We do not know when the crowner will return. He is hunting smugglers on the coast. In the meantime, Prioress Eleanor ordered me to examine the body immediately before rot destroyed any important details. Now, of course, we must find a messenger to search for him and bring him back."

The man raised his eyebrows. "Then I might be able to help you beyond the paltry information I have just provided. My own village, to which I am returning today, is on the East Anglian coast. Before I left there, I had heard rumors of these smugglers and that a king's man was coming to hunt them down. I assume this must be the crowner, although I grieve to hear that he has failed in this task. But it is likely I could find your crowner quickly. My neighbors and kin are sure to have heard of his current whereabouts."

Thomas felt an immense relief. Few men in Tyndal village had time to go off in search of the crowner when fields needed tending and market day was approaching for merchants. "With gratitude, I accept your help."

"What message should I give him?"

"Tell Crowner Ralf that Brother Thomas begs him to return to Tyndal village with all good speed because a murder has occurred on the king's road just outside the priory."

The man nodded. "I shall leave as soon as I settle what is owed with the innkeeper."

Thomas thanked the man, watched him hurry back to the village, then gestured for the lay brothers to take the corpse to the priory chapel. There, Sister Anne would have the privacy to use her immense medical expertise to see anything he might have missed.

With nothing left to amuse them, the small company of villagers dispersed back to their homes and work, eager to tell all they knew—or imagined—to their wives and friends.

CHAPTER TWENTY

"It has been too long," Eleanor said to Signy. "Ralf should have returned by now."

The innkeeper said nothing and stared with studied fascination at a spot high on the audience chamber wall.

"Gytha has heard from Ralf, but he mentioned nothing about the man who volunteered to find him or that he had learned about the murder."

"If a man has come with a message, Gytha can send him back with a plea for her husband to come home." Signy's gaze remained fixed on the wall.

"She was not at the manor when the messenger arrived, his visit was short, and he has left. Sibley relayed her father's love to her step-mother, but she was unaware of the added complications. It is not a child's duty to take on the responsibility of her elders." Eleanor was becoming increasingly annoyed with the innkeeper over her stubborn unwillingness to help. "Ralf did not say where he was on the coast."

"A man from the village can seek him out."

Eleanor lost the last of her patience. Signy had always been reasonable and eager to help when needed. Her current obstinacy was infuriating, and Eleanor found little reason for it other than sheer hardheadedness. She calmed herself, and her eyes narrowed. "Who can leave his shop or field right now?"

Signy threw her hand up and began to pace. "I know you want to send Nute, but I need his help in the inn as much as anyone else needs a husband, son, or brother on the farm or in the shop."

Eleanor walked over to her friend, put a hand on her shoulder, and forced her to stop walking.

The innkeeper did but refused to look Eleanor in the eye.

"Who best to go?" Eleanor said softly. "I know you need him, but Nute is reliable and clever. He can speak to Gytha. She must know someone he can ask in Norwich, where our crowner is based. Nute would not delay or be distracted. If he needs directions on where to go, he knows how to ask."

"I need him at the inn."

Eleanor sighed. "Why do you refuse? This is unlike you. I do not pretend that his absence for a few days would not be hard, but you have run the inn by yourself for years." She now turned to pleading. "The man who volunteered to find and tell Ralf that he must return has either chosen not to honor his word or could not find the crowner. I have tried to spare you—"

"I do not want to encourage him. Nute would love to go! He and I have quarreled of late over his desire to become one of Ralf's men. I explained several times why I need him to take responsibility for the inn and that it is his obligation to his sister, even more than it is any duty to me. Despite the love he bears Ingerith, he refuses and continues to rebel against my wishes by doing anything he can for Ralf. If I allow him to do this, he will think I am conceding to his desires."

"I had heard the rumor of a quarrel between you and your foster son. I did not know the cause."

Signy faced her, and Eleanor realized the woman was fighting back tears.

"Were his sister a lad," the innkeeper said, "I would not mind granting permission for Nute to follow his wish, but Ingerith is too young now to take on more responsibility, and her rights as a woman under the law do not protect her ownership of the inn when I die. Nute must take over and keep it safe for her."

Eleanor thought for a moment, then asked, "Is Ingerith eager to run the inn when she is able, even if the establishment remains in Nute's name?"

"She loves everything about it. I have no doubt she would continue it as a profitable business. But he must know how to do so when she marries and he must take on the work. I do not want the inn to become her husband's, even if he is a good man."

Eleanor understood exactly what she meant and reached out to take the innkeeper's hands. "Signy, I would not ask this boon of you if I could do otherwise. This murder is not within my authority. King Edward would have every right to protest my involvement to the Church because of the precedent it might set. For that reason, I dare not even send Brother Thomas to seek the crowner." She looked at Signy with a pleading expression. "If Ralf delays returning much longer, the murderer will probably escape or even kill again. I have done all I can, and yet our villagers have the right to feel confident that justice will be rendered and that they are safe from violence. It is crucial that Ralf be summoned home."

"You are kind not to tell me I am selfish, my lady."

"Your primary concern is not the profitability of your inn should Nute be gone for a few days. I know you better than that." She smiled. "And the reasons you gave me for your hesitancy are only part of your concern. As his mother, you worry about his safety wandering so far from home alone."

"He may be a man under the king's law. He is still a boy in my heart." The innkeeper wiped her eyes dry of tears.

Eleanor realized she was winning this argument. "Let Nute take the message to Ralf. Warn him about the dangers on the road and the precautions he must take. Phrase it not as a mother, but as one who is giving directions in how to reach his destination. The lad will listen. He is wiser than most of his age as well as being very clever."

Signy nodded, but her sorrow had not abated.

"When the perpetrator of this violence is found, or if Ralf decides nothing can be done, I will help you in this problem of your son's rebellion. I swear it."

The innkeeper's eyes narrowed. "I cannot give Nute what he wants."

"Set aside the argument for now. I beg you. Tell your son, if you must, that this will be the last time he can help the crowner. In the meantime, I shall pray for guidance. It is often in silence and peace that we find answers to difficult problems, not in the hurly-burly of shouts and anger."

"Then Nute may go. I shall send him to you," Signy replied and tried to smile. "I am truly grateful for your promise of a resolution. You have never failed us, my lady, and I welcome anything you can do." Her tone was honest even if her smile failed to be.

As Eleanor watched the innkeeper leave, she knew that she had no answer for the innkeeper's problem with her foster son. Looking across the room at her prie-dieu, she hoped God would grant her the needed wisdom, but deep in her soul she feared she might never find the answer promised without breaking the heart of one she cared about.

CHAPTER TWENTY-ONE

Sister Anne finished examining Gytha in the closed-off corner of the apothecary hut where she stored her medical books.

As she turned away from the crowner's wife, she glanced up at them, many of which were gifts from grateful patients, and a few were exceedingly rare. Although she had memorized most, she went over to her collection and fingered one, firmly chained to the wall, as if pondering a thought and wishing to research it further. In fact, she was stalling for time to think.

"You may tell me the truth, Sister. Must I prepare my husband and babes for my death?" Gytha's voice trembled.

Realizing now that the young woman had interpreted her act of turning away in silence as a dire diagnosis, Sister Anne looked around in horror. "You may be weak, Gytha, but not dying! Yes, you are frail, but there is no reason to be frightened. I only wanted to confirm that my thoughts on treatment were supported by those far wiser than I."

Her pallor fading, the crowner's wife bent forward to whisper, "Then may I confide in you a matter that is deeply troubling me? It may, I fear, be a wickedness." Seeing Sister Anne's guarded expression, she sat back. "Of course I shall confess to a priest, but I need to unburden my fears to you first. I believe you will understand and see how the problem weighs on my body as well as my soul, even though you will not approve."

"Then tell me. My ears lead only to a woman's heart and not to my tongue."

Gytha flushed and lowered her eyes. "My husband and I love our children. Each one is a joy to our lives, and God has blessed me with a fertility that allows us to bring more souls into this life to serve Him." Her voice faded into an uneasy silence.

During those years Sister Anne had been at her physician father's side and in the apothecary business with her husband, she had seen that look from many women and recognized the tone. The phrasing might vary, but Gytha had little new to add to the usual plea.

She encouraged Gytha to continue.

"After the last miscarriage, I grew weak. You can see that I have not regained my strength." She started at a sudden noise and looked over her shoulder but saw no one near. "My husband and I now fear lying together, a happiness that brought us contentment as well as earthly pleasure."

"You know I have been married to the man now called the Hermit of Tyndal?"

Gytha blinked. "I do."

"I only ask so you will know that I am not a stranger to the joys of the marriage bed." Nor was it a happiness she had ever wanted to reject. It was her husband who decided he must take vows after the death of their only child, believing the little boy had died as God's punishment for his own carnal lusts and not because their son had transgressed. She bit her lip, then said, "You may speak as one married woman to another."

The young woman still could not meet Sister Anne's eyes. "My husband fears that if we couple and I quicken, it will kill me. I also fear I will die in the next birthing and leave our babes without a mother." With her jaw set, she now looked up at Sister Anne. "Lest you think me completely selfish in this, I have told Ralf he must remarry and begged him to do so for his sake as well as that of our children. But he swears he will not, even if his brother demands it to enrich the family."

"For all your husband's faults, he is a man of honor who keeps his word. He would not have sworn that if he did not mean it."

"What can we do? Abstinence is destroying the joy in our marriage, and the Church has given its blessing for us to couple. Were I less fruitful, we might lie together without fearing it each time." Tears began to roll down her cheeks. "Is it so truly wicked to wish we had children less often? We both are happy to bring more into the world, if God wills it. I accept the curse of Eve in childbearing, but I find myself praying that it will not occur quite so often."

"You are not speaking of abortions?"

"I just suffered a miscarriage. It must have been God's will to end my pregnancy, but it certainly was not ours. Even without committing any sin, that loss caused us profound grief. My body has not recovered from the sorrow, and neither has my heart."

Sister Anne was satisfied, again turned her back, and pretended to study the volumes stored behind her. All she needed was time to remember what her father had taught her, the reasons he gave her for his decisions, and then carefully phrase an answer for Gytha.

This time, the crowner's wife knew that all she had to do was wait.

Sister Anne randomly selected one book and opened it at a page she pretended was relevant. When she noticed that it dealt with hives, she covered her mouth to keep from laughing. The humor of that moment actually brought her the needed clarity of thought. She closed the book, replaced it in the allotted space, and faced Gytha.

"There is one more thing that deeply troubles Ralf and me," the young woman murmured.

"Tell me."

"Sibley knows I am not well. She is now silent and withdrawn. Neither my husband nor I can make her laugh."

"Her mother died birthing her, yet she has loved you as if you had carried her in your own womb. Now she believes you may die as well. She cannot bear it."

"You do understand!"

Sister Anne nodded sadly. "She is not the first child to learn she cannot love too often because Death hovers so close. Priests counsel faith, but children rarely comprehend as an adult might, although even we often fail too or only succeed after great struggle. Wee ones bury the pain in the heart's secret place. As they grow older, they forget where that is but still feel the deep ache. To my knowledge, no one has ever found the place where it is hidden."

"What shall we do?"

"You have been both cursed and blessed with great fertility. Your fears are not unusual. All I am able to offer you, however, is the healing of your body," Sister Anne said. "A priest must teach you how to bear any other burden you have been given."

Gytha's shoulders sagged, and she looked at Sister Anne with sad acceptance.

"But heal you, I may. It will take time, but I have found a regimen that can bring your strength back. Fortunately, God has gifted you with a body strong enough to have borne three healthy boys, and you have had only two miscarriages. I believe this treatment is not too late and will be successful."

"I shall do all you ask." The crowner's wife straightened her back with determined resignation.

As she prepared to give her the same advice she had given other women, Sister Anne prayed Gytha would listen carefully and obey precisely. No method was perfect, but this was one her father had found to be the most successful as long as the procedure was followed carefully.

She began her discussion with the conventional advice about diet and exercise, all in moderation. Then she walked over to a shelf and pulled down a jar, setting it on the table.

"My next instructions are probably the most important part in regaining your health. You must listen carefully and follow my instructions exactly. If there is something you do not understand, you must ask me. It is also crucial that Ralf knows every detail of this regime, and he should come to me for direction. It is as important that your husband cooperate fully in this treatment as it is for you, or it will not work."

Perhaps there was an odd tone in her stern voice that caused Gytha's eyes to widen. But if she noticed anything unusual, she chose not to betray her thoughts.

"First, you and your husband must practice abstinence until after you have suffered two full courses."

"I have just finished one, and we had not coupled for some time before. Ralf has been on the coast hunting smugglers, and he does not know when he will return."

"You may count this last one." Sister Anne smiled. "With Ralf away, the remaining time may not be as difficult for you both."

Gytha blushed.

The nun put a hand on the jar she had taken down. "This contains seeds from the wild carrot." She poured a small quantity of the brownish seeds into her hand and showed it to the crowner's wife. "I will grind them just enough to make the dose easier to chew and swallow, but this is the amount you must take. Memorize what you see. When you chew them, the taste will be unpleasantly oily, so you may drink it down with a little ale or wine. I will give you a supply from the jar, which you must take as I direct. Request more from me before you take the last dose."

As she explained how many days Gytha must take the dose after lying with her husband, how long the hiatus might be, and when she must start the treatment again, the young woman concentrated on every detail. Each direction she repeated or rephrased to make sure she understood. She even asked how well to chew the roughly ground seeds and how many swallows of the drink were needed to take them with.

"Not only will this treatment with wild carrot return you to health, it is especially efficacious in providing a woman with the continued strength to endure quickening when such occurs. That is why you must follow the directed routine exactly. You and Ralf may return to the joys of your marriage bed, although abstinence is wise from time to time. If you suspect you have become pregnant, see me right away."

"This must be continued indefinitely?"

Sister Anne nodded. "Each year, I must examine you. It is often wise to make adjustments in the routine, and we shall discuss that each time."

Gytha stared at her, then ran one hand under her eyes as if to chase away tears. "It improves health that much?"

"No herb or potion can substitute for God's will, but my father learned the benefits of wild carrot from ancient texts, such as the works of Hippocrates, and discussed its actual success with those wise physicians from whom he learned much."

Sister Anne quickly made up a box of packets and handed it to the young woman. "When you need more, come to me. If I am not here, ask Sister Oliva. No one else."

With a trembling hand, Gytha took the box. "You have given me hope, Sister. How can Ralf and I ever thank you?"

"Pray for me," Sister Anne replied, "for I am a weak and sinful woman." She bowed her head.

Hesitating, Gytha took in a breath as if she wanted to say something further, then chose to leave without doing so.

Only when she heard the young woman's steps fade away did Sister Anne raise her head. She sat down on the bench, still warm from where the crowner's wife had sat, and stared at the jar of wild carrot seed.

She knew that Gytha had understood exactly what the remedy she had given her was for. Had she gravely sinned and led an innocent into the same transgression, or would God agree that she had followed one of His principles of which even the Church approved?

Her father believed the latter was true.

In her mind, she heard her father's words, spoken as if he were standing next to her, his voice as deep and gentle as she remembered: "In a difficult birth, the Church allows us to save a mother's life over that of her child should a choice be necessary. So when I give a weakened woman and her husband this remedy to preserve her health, I follow the spirit of those teachings. In doing so, I often save two lives, hers and that of a child who might innocently kill her and then die as well. In my soul, I do not believe that God condemns me. Yet you must know that when I said this to our priest, he rebuked me and insisted I had committed a profound sin. When I begged him for an explanation of the difference, all he said was that my act was the Devil's work."

When she was old enough to question him further, she asked, "Then why not give all married couples this remedy?"

"If a woman is not in poor health," he had replied, "I find no justification for doing so. Only pagans and other non-believers say that hindering the seed of a man and woman from joining together is not always wicked."

His voice now faded, and Sister Anne missed him with fresh sorrow. She knew, as did others, that his medical sources were not all Christian, including the circle of men he often consulted. Knowing this, some afflicted had refused all his treatments because they feared the source of the cure was tainted by non-believers. Others had trusted God to have cleansed the treatment of sin and concluded that was why he was such a skilled healer. But her father had believed God had given men intelligence and the ability to reason for good cause, and she believed the same.

Rising, she replaced the jar in its allotted spot and glanced heavenward. Would her father have been pleased that she had changed the usage of the wild carrot from what he advised based on her own observations? Or would he conclude she had offended God?

Conventional wisdom said that a woman was most fertile after her courses, yet Sister Anne had noticed that conception seemed to take place more often when the seeds were joined just before. The only time she had quickened with a living child was such an instance.

And thus she began suggesting that a woman start the dosages a couple of weeks after she last needed grass to absorb her blood flow. Since she was going against established medical wisdom, she wondered at first if God might be more willing to forgive her because her advice about when to use wild carrot to prevent pregnancy was so clearly in error. That hope vanished after it became clear that her method was very successful.

As she left the apothecary hut to return to her rounds of the sick in the hospital, she knew she would have to confess to a priest that she had again sinned by offering advice on how to reduce births. Yet her success did not seem to matter. When the priests learned that trained doctors insisted she was wrong about the likely time of conception, the confessor always gave her a lesser penance. Wicked though her motives might be, she must inevitably fail because of her medical ignorance.

CHAPTER TWENTY-TWO

Ralf frowned.

Gracia poured him more ale.

Tired though he was, he smiled and thanked her.

"The original messenger said his home was on the coast," Brother Thomas said. "I had no reason to question that. He seemed confident that he could find you."

"That certainty was not unreasonable. It is difficult to hide a band of men who have been revisiting the same areas of coastline where smugglers might land. We had to buy supplies. One of our men fell sick and needed care..." Ralf suddenly glowered. "I pray no one paid this messenger for his efforts! I fear he may have lied to you for gain."

"No, nor did he ask for it. He said he was returning anyway. Seeking your whereabouts seemed to be no inconvenience to him," Thomas said.

Ralf sank thoughtfully into silence, then said, "It troubles me that I never saw him."

"I failed to ask his name, nor did I learn the name of his village, and for those omissions I beg pardon." Thomas looked more than sorry. He looked like a judge about to condemn a man to the gallows, only he was the felon as well as the judge.

"Give me a description of the man. Perhaps my men saw him in one of the villages or on the road, but he did not recognize them."

"Dark hair that peaked down his forehead. Stocky. Big ears. Skin tanned from much sun, but unpitted by the pox. A scar over his left eye." He thought for a moment, then shook his head.

"That sounds like Warin! He is a Norwich man though, not from the coastal villages. Nor would he be known in Tyndal. He was part of my company at the keep and had never come here."

"I thought he had a Norwich accent," Thomas said.

"I sent him back to the city to hunt down wool merchants who might be involved in the smuggling. Yet it could not have been him. Why would he come here?" Scratching his chin, he added, "Do you recall if he had any teeth missing?"

Thomas took only a moment to think, then pointed to two of his own. "He did. These in front."

"Must be Warin, but I still do not understand..."

Eleanor, who had been silent until now, said, "He may have found your merchant and followed him if the man left Norwich on business."

"You may well be right," Ralf said, then squeezed his eyes shut as if they stung.

"Yet the dead man couldn't have been that merchant. He did not seem to know him and said only that he had briefly shared a table with the fellow at Signy's inn. Apparently, the dead man spoke little and was not part of any group."

"Warin would not have revealed that he had been following him nor said he knew him at all. But now I fear someone saw him, a man who had cause to stop him before he reached me. I fear he may be in danger or has already suffered tragically for his knowledge." Ralf shut his eyes again, and a few tears wandered down his cheeks.

"You need to go home, Ralf," Eleanor said. "Seeing your family and sleeping well tonight will help much."

"I am tired..." He looked as if he might fall asleep where he sat.

"And worried about your wife. I know. We have spoken."

His look revealed all his fears as well as his fatigue, but Eleanor knew she mustn't speak of it.

Taking a deep breath and straightening his shoulders, Ralf replied, "I am grateful you were willing to help with this murder as soon as it happened, my lady. It was not your responsibility, and yet your swift action has gained information that would have been lost otherwise."

"Yet I fear the killer has left the village," she said.

He nodded. "I have two problems now. This murder will be addressed, but I must also find out what has happened to Warin. He knew where I was, yet I have not seen him. I have concluded that this smuggling operation is too well organized for just one man to be leading it. Someone may have followed Warin and killed him before he could bring me word."

"We have always worked well together, Ralf," Eleanor said. "May I suggest a solution to this problem?"

His smile may have been thin, but it conveyed an honest gratitude.

"Go back to the coast, if you feel that might help you find Warin, and try to find out what happened to him."

He nodded. "We might simply have missed each other. He could not have seen any of my men before either. He and they would have recognized each other. If God is kind, Warin is now with them and waiting for me..." Ralf realized he was thinking out loud to no point and asked the prioress to continue.

"While you do that, Brother Thomas can question any pilgrims still at the inn who were here at the time of the murder. Perhaps someone recalls something useful about the victim. I doubt any of the villagers had much if any contact with the pilgrims, so questioning them might not be useful. Concentrating on those at the inn, the serving women most certainly, should be our best hope for information. Signy is very observant herself."

Ralf shook his head. "I can understand asking the wenches and Signy, but why would there be any pilgrims remaining who had met or spoken to the dead man?"

"Traveling parties get separated. Some pilgrims might wait for family members to catch up. Illness would be another reason. We have had a few pilgrims come to our hospital." She smiled. "The occasional baby has been born."

Eleanor sat back and briefly let Ralf struggle with that logic, his drooping eyes losing the battle as he fought back sleep.

What she especially chose not to include was her suspicion that the beating of the carpenter might be connected to the murder. If so, this might be a much more complex situation than the killing of the merchant, and the perpetrator had remained in the inn far longer than the average pilgrim. Why might he have done so? Who might have noticed this traveler, who stayed overlong and looked like a pilgrim, and hopefully recalled some pertinent details? Or, as she feared, had the murderer left by now?

In any case, her monk should start a thorough investigation at the inn immediately, and if there was a connection between the two violent acts, Brother Thomas might help the crowner solve the murder, the beating, and perhaps even help find a solution to the smuggling.

Ralf brightened. "Catching the killer here is probably impossible, but Brother Thomas may find out enough for me to pursue the man." He winked at the monk. "'Tis a pity you took vows, Brother. The king would welcome a man like you to render his justice. Perhaps he will meet you one day and thank you personally for the service you have given him."

Thomas shivered in the warm room and hoped the crowner didn't see it. The last thing he wanted to do was see the king. Edward might recognize in his face that young boy, bastard son of a high-ranking man, who later fell into Hell but was then allowed to vanish into a remote priory that smelled of rank seaweed and rotting fish.

As he stood, Ralf suddenly learned against the table as if he had lost his balance.

"Go home, Ralf." Eleanor gestured at the door of her audience chamber. "Out!"

He nodded, fatigue deepening the wrinkles in his forehead and hollowing out his eyes. "I promise to follow up on every lead you find."

"Of course you will." Eleanor nodded to Thomas. "Take this man home, Brother. I do not want him to fall asleep in mid-stride, tumble into the stream, and drown."

The crowner did not even have the strength to argue as Thomas led him from the chamber.

After closing the door behind the two men, Gracia looked at Eleanor with admiration. "You were kind to give Brother Thomas leave to go with him."

Eleanor understood that most prioresses would not have done so. "His wife would never forgive me if he didn't arrive home safely," she replied and then laughed. "But our Ralf may not be so grateful when he faces her wrath over how exhausted he has let himself become."

CHAPTER TWENTY-THREE

When Thomas had first arrived at Tyndal Priory, he initially suspected Brother John of having committed a brutal crime. In return, Brother John had taken an instant dislike, bordering on revulsion, to the reluctant monk who had entered holy service without religious vocation.

But they had grown to respect each other over time despite being very different men. They were first surprised when they bonded over a shared joy in music. Eventually, each realized that the other had suffered some profound wound that had never healed. As Brother John continued his determined journey to completely escape the world, Thomas gave him support, although his own attempt to do the same had failed. John may not have known the source of Thomas's agony, but he respected how he rejected the easy path of attacking others in anger or retaliation for his pain and instead had chosen to gently serve those in need. They never spoke to each other of what they had discovered. There was no need to do so.

Thomas, like his prioress, had picked John as his confessor. Despite the hermit's own self-hatred, he felt compassion for the worldly frailties of others, especially the weaknesses of men, and his required penances were rigorous but both fair and wise.

This was why Thomas now knelt in front of the skeletal Hermit of Tyndal and sobbed without restraint.

Only under duress had Thomas ever spoken about his longing to lie with other men since he was released from prison and forced to have his head shaved for a tonsure. His confessions remained general about lust in dreams or how his arms ached to hold the warm body of someone loved in a way that was far less spiritual than physical. This time he told the hermit every detail.

By the end, his soul was bleeding. The effort hurt more than any penitential whiplash against his body. The most difficult part was Brother John's silence. Had Thomas been condemned as Satan's minion, he would have understood. But he did not know the meaning of such stillness or the steady gaze of the hermit's green eyes.

When he spoke about his encounter with the merchant on the Welsh border, John said nothing, nor did he scowl, nor did he lean away in horror.

When Thomas explained that he had almost let the merchant pleasure him until his seed released yet fled before that ultimate sin had been committed, tears bathed the hermit's cheeks.

At the end of the grueling confession, Thomas kept his eyes closed out of terror. Surely the quiet in the room presaged a wrath that would burn him to ash. Or was Satan rushing to rip his soul out with sharpened claws and toss it into hellfire?

When Thomas finally gained the courage to open his eyes, the hermit was leaning back, those unsettling green eyes staring upward, as if he were listening to a celestial voice.

Thomas said nothing, although the stillness in the hut weighed down on him like an ever growing pile of stones. He found it hard to breathe. Was this God's way of killing him?

"Brother Thomas," the hermit finally whispered, "you have gravely offended God."

Although barely audible, that murmur sounded like the trumpet on Judgment Day to Thomas.

"Yet you struggled. You fled the Devil's arms. This proves to God that you love Him more than Satan or any earthly pleasure."

Thomas knew that wasn't true. It was not thoughts of God that had saved him from the ultimate sin. Had the man caressing him been Durant, he probably would have cast all qualms aside that night. He remembered he would have been willing enough to go to Hell holding the wine merchant in his arms.

"I cannot claim any such virtue," Thomas said.

"God can read the state of your soul better than you."

Thomas had no response. What could God have seen that was any different from what he recalled from that night in the shadowed close?

"A man's body is a foul and evil thing," the hermit continued. "In dreams, we release our seed because Satan knows how weak we are in sleep. Then the creature gives us the waters of Lethe to drink so we forget what it was in the dream that caused us to fall from grace. Thus we cannot gird our loins to fight against it in the future."

Thomas did not agree. For a long time, it was the memory of the body of that man he had first loved that drove him to such lust that he awakened from his dreams with an orgasmic scream of joy.

The expression on the hermit's face softened into a more pensive look. "Some saints say we must tie our genitals down before sleep, but I have not found that helpful. Others argue that we should castrate ourselves." He thought for a moment. "I believe that was Origen?"

Thomas felt himself grow numb with fear and ardently prayed that the hermit would not demand that penance. It was hard enough to accept that Durant had suffered the mutilation.

"Maybe some men do find favor with God by gelding themselves, but I believe it is a rare act and may even be sinful."

Thomas let out his breath.

"After much prayer in the solitude of this hut, I have grown increasingly confident that God believes the penance must fit both the sin and the man. As He has guided me to give up the world, it is equally clear that He requires you to remain in it to help our prioress. And thus I believe that you must find your penance in an example from the life of our founder, Robert of Arbrissel."

"I beg you to explain."

"Did he not go into the houses where whores lay with men for coin? Did he not preach righteousness to the Magdalenes, even as they reeked of their squalid beds? Never once did he falter despite the temptations they offered. He left the brothels with his virtue intact yet converted whores who followed him to a godly life. He faced a man's greatest fear and weakness but conquered all to God's glory."

"Such is indeed the tale we are told." Yet my greatest weakness is not lust for women, Thomas thought. After I took vows, I no longer wanted to lie with them.

As if reading Thomas's mind, the hermit smiled. "You fled the man whose body Satan had entered to tempt you into one of the vilest of transgressions. You showed God that the Evil One might seduce you, but you refused to give him your ultimate fealty."

"I might not be so strong another time."

The hermit nodded. "Are you familiar with the tale of how Robert the Devil cast forth his evil nature because he loved God more?"

"The Anchoress Juliana told me to read it."

"Do you recall the most important elements of his redemption?"

"I have not yet sought the tale from our library and know only what our anchoress told me."

"Robert sought the advice of a holy man, who told him that he could cleanse his soul if he spent years of excruciating penance during which he would endure all forms of pain, but must do so in utter silence. He became a mute slave until the day came when the holy man released him from his vows. Then Robert forsook the world and the love of a good woman to become a hermit and later a saint."

Thomas frowned. "I have already taken vows, and I shall never be a saint. How can I follow this example? How can God ever forgive a man as thoroughly wicked as I? Robert the Devil's soul was given to Satan by his mother. It was not his wish. He had the right to beg mercy with his own voice. I do not have his excuse."

"You have forgotten, Brother, that all men are born into sin, but we are also made in God's image. If you are able to grieve over your frailty, you may hope for God's compassion. You are His creature after all. It is only those who wallow with delight in wickedness and claim virtue they do not have whom He will cast into the abyss."

Thomas had no strength to argue further and only wanted to hear what the hermit deemed a proper penance.

"You must muse daily on the example of our founder's strength and how he triumphed over a man's willful nature and sinful body, as did Robert the Devil. You will be tempted constantly to lie with a man but shall learn not to succumb. You will suffer agonies but find no earthly remedy. In facing your weakness, you, like our founder, will eventually discover how to love with a pure heart. In this way, you will find peace and forgiveness. You will be cleansed of sin."

Thomas bowed his head in submission but still failed to understand the details of his penance, other than the meditation on the acts of Robert of Arbrissel and the penance of a man whose tale he had yet to read.

"You have told me about Durant the vintner, who will be coming to Tyndal and has begged for your care and guidance. You fear that you will blacken his chances at Heaven instead."

"That is my fear."

"I suspect he may also be a man who tempts you?"

Thomas stared at him with icy horror.

"You have not said so, but I have heard the warmth in your voice when you speak his name."

Thomas looked away and felt his face burn. How many others had read his feelings so easily?

"Your penance, therefore, is to care for this man who tempts you but who was brutally castrated. You will be tempted by lust but denied any earthly pleasure. You will learn to care lovingly but without wickedness. With dedicated struggle, your lusts will die, and you will only long to ease him into Heaven. That, Brother Thomas, is your penance until God takes the soul of Master Durant."

Can I? Thomas wondered. Or will I find some other way to dance with the Devil, as I did with Lambard?

"Your tears when you knelt before me and begged confession do you credit," the hermit said. "If you did not feel deep remorse for your sins, you would not have done so. I am convinced you hold out your hand to God and long to rid yourself of wickedness." He put a hand on the monk's shoulder, then put his finger on Thomas' forehead and sketched a sign of the cross. "Go back to the priory, Brother, obey God's laws, and serve your penance with strength of purpose and humble obedience."

Thomas remained on his knees until calm, wiped his cheeks dry, then rose unsteadily.

The hermit took Thomas's arm and led him to the open door. Without further word, Brother John left him there and went back to his altar and his own agonized prayers.

Thomas stepped outside and blinked as the hot sun burned his tender eyes, lacerated by salty tears. Finding the path that went down to the stream where he used to swim during the year when he was known as the Hermit of Tyndal, he slowly descended. Halfway there, he stopped for a moment to listen to the silence that surrounded the place, a peace he sometimes regretted he had chosen to leave.

And yet he had more profoundly missed serving his prioress in that search for justice which God demanded of her. Gently pressing his stinging eyes, he wondered if God might look on him with a little favor because of his paltry contributions to those quests. Maybe there is hope, he thought, and perhaps God had directed the hermit to offer me a way to avoid Hell.

His strength had vanished after the strain of his confession. He longed to find a small patch of sun and a soft bed of leaves where he could sleep. Yet he knew he must go without further delay to the inn, as he had promised Prioress Eleanor.

"All I need is just another moment to regain my strength," he whispered to the insects now whirring invisibly in the dim shade.

He knelt on the path and looked down into the brook rushing past him. A silvery fish leapt out of the water, flashed in the sunlight, and plunged back into the stream. Thomas smiled, sat down, and stared into the swift, gurgling water that had so often cooled his body during that year in the hut where Brother John now lived.

One more moment, he thought, I need just one more moment.

Despite the sound of the murmuring water, Thomas again heard the hermit's voice echoing in his soul.

Brother John had promised that he did have a choice between Hell and Heaven. He was not without hope of mercy. The penance required for the sin Thomas had committed would be hard, but he also believed that it came with the promise of God's forgiveness. He would perform it for Durant's sake. Any further doubts or temptations he would take to the altar, and beg for answers that sometimes were granted.

Rising, Thomas climbed back up the hill to the main road and walked swiftly to the inn.

CHAPTER TWENTY-FOUR

Oswin emerged into the sweet warmth of the sun. Despite his battered body, his spirit felt as joyful and eager as a boy running out to play.

"How quickly we forget the innocent pleasures of childhood," he whispered to himself, then lifted his face with closed eyes to savor that brief moment when life felt wonderfully uncomplicated.

The widow emerged and quickly caught up with him.

"If you tire, let me know," she said, a deep furrow in her forehead suggesting she had not approved of this decision to venture out.

He grinned. "If I do, then you will have to carry me back to bed."

She blushed.

Instantly, he regretted his brash remark. She was a kind woman, had cared for him well, and did not deserve that unintended suggestion of impropriety. "Of course I did not mean that you should do so by yourself, Mistress Hilde. Seek Nute at the inn, and he will send men from there to assist me."

She nodded, but her frown disappeared. "This walk is against the advice of the priory lay brother."

"What do monks know of worldly men who must earn their bread with the strength of their bodies, not the stoutness of their souls? I must regain my strength. I have work to finish for the innkeeper. Not only did I give her my word I would do it, I need the coin if I am to return home."

"Your wife and babes must miss you."

For a moment, he feared tears would betray him, but, with gritted teeth, he banished them. "No longer, mistress. While I was gone, they died of a cruel fever." His innocent enjoyment of the world around him now vanished, but the sun had remained kind and still granted him warmth. For that small gift, he was grateful.

"Surely you have other family who long for your return." Her voice was so soft it soothed as much as the sunshine.

"I have no one, but I must go back. I have a debt I must pay."

"After you have done so, why not return here? The village lacks a man of your skills, and Mistress Signy has praised your expertise and hard work." She bowed her head so he could not read her soul through her eyes.

For just an instant, he felt a burst of hope. Perhaps he could survive all that he must do to bring justice to those he loved and who had been so viciously left to die. He would never forget his sweet wife and tender daughter, but he had found some peace in this village. Might he be allowed to forget that he was a murderer, at least from the tolling of one church bell to the next?

But his heart froze, and the sun ceased to warm him. What a fool he was to think there was any realistic expectation that he could stop recalling his sins so easily, even from one Office to another. The guilt would always fester, and the bitterness would one day kill him if the hangman didn't.

"If you still insist on this walk," the widow said with mock severity, "then let us do so lest exhaustion strike you before you move from where you now stand."

Without any hint of mockery in return, he bowed his head to her and gestured that he was ready for the planned foray into the town square.

As they slowly walked past the old baker, the new glover, and the young smithy, the sun teased the pair into the ease of contentment.

Their conversation grew companionable. She smiled and jested with him. Once again, he relaxed. Had a stranger met them, he might have assumed they were long-married, a fortunate couple who had found a pleasant comfort with each other.

But even on the brightest days, clouds often dimmed the sun. As the pair began to return to the inn, Oswin laughed at something the widow had said, then he stumbled to a stop.

The red-haired monk from the priory was walking into the inn.

Is he looking for me? Oswin wondered as he willed himself not to tremble. Has he discovered who I am?

Although the man was a religious, Oswin knew Brother Thomas was hardly innocent of worldly matters. The monk's reputation was well-known, and anyone who thought him a fool would be bitterly disappointed.

"I fear you were right from the beginning, mistress," he said, now uncontrollably shivering. "I have suddenly grown very weak."

Her merriness vanished, and she grasped his arm with worry. "Are you strong enough to wait here until I can summon a man to come to your aid?"

He shook his head. "That is not needed. I only meant that we should take the short way back to my cell. I can walk that distance with your help alone."

"It is not a cell," she said as they traveled slowly across the square. "It is a place of healing."

The slip had been unintentional, and he was grateful that she did not grasp the full implication of what he had said. Yet Oswin knew he had meant to use the word. His soul was imprisoned, although his body might still be unfettered.

How soon, he asked himself, before I am caught and led to the gallows?

CHAPTER TWENTY-FIVE

Nute rushed to greet Thomas when he walked through the inn door.

"How may I help you, Brother?"

Thomas quickly exchanged his spontaneous grin for a more serious mien. The lad's eagerness was akin to that of a puppy anticipating a rare treat, but he did not want Nute to think he was mocking his enthusiasm because it was boyish. In truth, he was pleased and willing enough to treat him with the seriousness due a man.

Although he knew that Signy was opposed to the lad's desire to help Ralf, Thomas had long appreciated how the crowner lovingly treated Nute as if he were his own son. It was an experience Thomas had lacked as a boy, and his heart always warmed when he saw men who showed boys a father's affection. As much as he respected the innkeeper, Thomas was on the side of her foster son in this. He understood how much Nute longed to please the man who gave him the paternal love he needed.

Thomas took the youth by the arm and directed him to a quieter part of the inn. "Crowner Ralf has need of our assistance," he murmured.

Had Nute been a few years younger, he might have jumped up and down with the thrill of hearing those words. As a lad with one leg just over the fence into manhood, he managed to keep his delight to the sparkle in his eyes.

"Will your mother mind if I steal a little of your time to ask some questions?"

Immediately, Nute looked around to see where Signy was. Once he knew she was not in the area, he folded his arms and struck a pose. It was a fine attempt at appearing adult. "She never minds when I talk with you, Brother."

"Yet I shall be brief. Will you discreetly point out which customers have remained here since the beating of the carpenter? And do you know why they have stayed so long?"

Nute quickly pointed out the few who had, and the reasons he gave for staying proved common enough: illness or rest for an aged pilgrim, waiting for delayed family members or friends, and one merchant had decided to do a little profitable business on the way home.

"Only one man troubles me, Brother." The youth tilted his head in the direction of a man sitting alone in a far corner of the inn.

Thomas glanced at him, then moved his direct gaze away and smiled as he pretended to appreciate how a serving wench carried several pitchers of ale without spilling a drop. But from the corner of his eye, he continued to study the man. He seemed restless, switching his mazer from hand to hand, then rubbing his face with his hands. Or was he merely bored?

"Why does he trouble you?" Thomas now turned his attention to the other side of the inn where two local men were engaged in a heated conversation that only friends could have without danger of violence. He knew them and expected one would soon laugh and clap the other on his back. A jack of ale would be drunk, and the men would eventually leave and return to whatever task they had been avoiding.

"I hadn't paid much attention to him before Oswin's beating," Nute said, "but I did after. He always sat with two other men, one of them the man who was killed. I thought the dead man was a merchant and that the man over there was his servant. The two were also in the

company of a third man, who has since left." He hesitated. "I fear some
of this I should have told Prioress Eleanor when I begged her help
after the man's murder. I was frightened that my foster mother would
be angry over my delay…"

"You are telling me now, and that is timely enough," Thomas said
to soothe the lad. What Nute said was troubling. This observation was
in conflict with what he had been told by the man Ralf called Warin.
"The dead man commonly sat with two other men? Was this his habit,
or did he usually sit by himself or even with a larger group for meals?"

"Sitting with just those two was his usual practice. It is possible
there was another merchant who joined a crowd as you describe, but I
do not recall that."

Thomas never liked such significant discrepancies in stories.
Perhaps this needed no resolution, but only Warin could explain, and
he had left to find the crowner. "Why do you think the dead man was
a merchant and that man his servant?"

"I decided to train my ability to observe detail when I served them.
The dead man's attire was made of fine cloth, although his speech was
not that of a highborn man. The man still here was attentive to him,
but not like a casual acquaintance met on the road. He was alert to
moods and needs as a servant would be. His cloak was made of rough
cloth, yet now he wears a robe. It is similar to that of the dead man but
much more worn. I suspect he took one of his master's lesser
garments after he died. Perhaps to disguise his own humble rank?"
Nute stopped. "Have I said anything of use?"

Thomas nodded encouragement to continue.

"The trio was an odd group." He blushed. "That was why I was
curious about them. From bits of conversation I overheard, I
concluded the dead man was likely a wool merchant. As I explained,
the man still here acted like his servant. If he was not, he was clearly
of lower status and accustomed to serve. As for the man who left, I
could not quite place his rank. He did not seem to have been on
pilgrimage, yet his bearing was not that of either master or servant."
Nute stopped to think. "Maybe they shared some common background, all being from Norwich?"

Thomas started as if he had unexpectedly been pricked with a sharp object. "Norwich? Wool merchant, you say?"

"The merchant talked about the wool trade. At some point, he also said something about them all traveling back to Norwich, and I recognized the accent." He grinned. "There are advantages to working in an inn, Brother. I may never have left Tyndal village, but much of the isle has traveled to me."

As he returned the lad's smile, that nagging noise in his head finally grew clear, and Thomas realized why he thought the corpse had looked familiar. The man who had approached him for a blessing when he first arrived at Durant's door had been going on pilgrimage to honor St. Walstan. That man and the corpse were the same.

"Your details are important, lad. I am proud of you." Thomas slapped the youth on the shoulder. The compliment was meant. The youth's observations were impressive.

Nute glowed with happiness.

Now Thomas had a dilemma. Was Ralf still here, or had he kissed his wife and children, then hurried back up the coast early today? Dare he take the time to go to the crowner's manor to see if the man was gone? And, if he had left Thomas knew he couldn't delay the next move until someone got word to Ralf that Thomas knew where the dead man resided and that the man's servant was still here.

Nor could he wait until the crowner either came back or sent word that he was unable to do so. This possible witness, or even one involved in the crime, might disappear at any moment. Prompt action was obligatory.

If Thomas learned something crucial from the servant, Prioress Eleanor could keep the man briefly locked up in the priory cell. Ralf would never object to her trespassing on the king's legal rights. She had friends of high rank in the court and could thus avoid most secular critics if anyone learned of her actions and, to gain the king's favor, chose to protest the overstepping of her rights.

Glancing back at the solitary man in the corner, Thomas decided on a plan.

"Can you watch the man while I question others who have also been here for the pertinent time?" He bent closer to Nute's ear. "Do whatever your mother requires of you. I need your help and do not want you to get into trouble. I must know if the man is only curious about a monk talking to people at an inn or if he displays some nervousness while I do so."

"I can bring ale and sell meals, Brother. The serving women always appreciate my help when we are busy." He chuckled. "The men prefer a prettier sight at their tables than I can offer, but my foster mother is pleased when I clean up or bring an extra pitcher or bowl of stew." He sighed. "She thinks I am showing interest in running the inn."

Thomas tapped the lad on his shoulder in appreciation, then headed for the first couple of pilgrims.

CHAPTER TWENTY-SIX

Nute had served so many tables and hovered very eagerly over others that a few too many patrons had drunk more ale than they might otherwise have done. Some even jestingly asked if he was urging food and drink on them because the stew was either going bad or the ale was. The latter were local men who knew full well that Signy never served anything that wasn't perfect and were fond enough of her foster son to tease him.

As he returned their banter, Nute watched the man he had promised to keep under observation. He even approached him, but only once, and asked if he wanted anything more to eat or drink.

The man froze at his approach like a cat hiding from a large hunting dog, and he paled as if every nerve ached with fear.

Nute gave him his broadest smile and temptingly presented a jug of ale.

This show of innkeeper pleasantry was greeted with a surly growl, despite the pallor, and a dismissive wave of the hand.

Nute swiftly went on to other customers.

&

Brother Thomas chatted amiably with those who had remained, beginning with ones seated farthest from his true quarry.

He learned that one young couple had gone to the priory hospital when the wife feared she was miscarrying, but that had been averted and they were now able to leave early the next morning.

An old man praised Sister Anne for helping him ease his gout. He passed Thomas a coin in gratitude.

A third man was well into his cups and ranted loudly about his best friend stealing his wife. A woman at a neighboring table gestured to Thomas to come closer and whispered that the wife had gotten tired of her husband's drunkenness and departed the inn with her brother.

The merchant, who had seen a chance for profit and stayed on, patted his plumper purse but offered no coin of gratitude to God, claiming he must now spend more for protection on the way home.

As Thomas slowly circled closer to the man of interest, he noticed that his prey seemed to shrink closer to the wall as if hoping to slip through it and escape notice. Wondering if he had somehow frightened the man too soon, Thomas deliberately turned away and began a conversation with another group of pilgrims who had recently arrived.

Meanwhile, Nute stood near the door opening into the kitchen area and scowled with authority. He might not have wanted to run this inn, but he did his best to look like he did.

Suddenly, a serving girl ran to him and begged his help. When she had tried to put a pitcher of ale on the table, one of the men had accidentally knocked it out of her hand.

Nute immediately went to the man, assuring him that no one would be charged for the spill, and ordered a fresh pitcher. The man was content, but the serving girl was young and insisted on pleading that she was not at fault for the incident. It was her first job, and she was frightened.

Nute tried to convince her that she would neither lose her job nor be asked to pay for the spill, but soothing took longer than expected. By the time she had calmed enough to return to her duties, and he had picked up a jug of ale to take on another round of the inn, Nute realized that the man he was supposed to be watching was no longer sitting where he had been.

Stunned with fear, Nute looked around.

The man was just fleeing through the inn door.

Slamming the jug down on a nearby table and telling the customers it was a gift from the innkeeper, Nute raced after him.

By the time he reached the door, the man had crossed the town square.

"He is headed for the road to Norwich!" Nute muttered.

He had no time to alert Brother Thomas about where he was going, nor could he say anything to his mother, who would refuse permission for him to follow were he to tell her.

There were too many places on that road where a man could disappear, Nute knew, and he could not let that happen.

With no further hesitation, he fled the inn, followed the man out of the village as carefully as possible, and down the road.

CHAPTER TWENTY-SEVEN

Thomas tried to comfort a man who had just buried his grandfather. At least he died after the pilgrimage with his soul at peace, the younger man said, but now he feared his own grieving was a sin. Shouldn't he be rejoicing instead? Thomas hoped he was able to assure him that mortal grief was understandable, even if the deceased was now sitting in the loving hand of God.

As he turned toward another table, however, Thomas saw that the man he had been circling was no longer seated where he had been.

With a swift glance around the room, he realized that Nute had also vanished.

Then he saw something that was even more unnerving.

Hands on hips, Signy was staring at the open inn door with an expression that would terrify a storm cloud rumbling to the coast from the land of eternal ice.

"What has the lad done?" Thomas muttered and hurried to her side.

"Have you seen him?" Signy said when he approached. She did not need to clarify the subject of her question.

"He was standing just there when I last saw him." Pointing to the kitchen entry, Thomas knew his face was hot with guilt. Whatever sympathy he had for Nute's longing, he was still a boy, and Thomas knew he was wrong to involve the lad without checking with his foster mother first.

Signy turned and touched the arm of an older woman who was carrying two bowls of stew. "Have you seen my son?"

"He left the inn but a moment ago," the woman said. "He was in a hurry." Then she looked at Thomas. "I thought he was on an errand for you, Brother."

Signy's lips quivered with rage, but her eyes also glistened with fear. "What has he done, Brother?"

"He is in no danger," he replied. "I will find him and bring him back."

She arched one black eyebrow.

Thomas fled the inn as if Satan himself were chasing him.

He did not find Nute.

A villager said he had seen the youth walking toward the road that took travelers from the village to Norwich.

Thomas immediately ran that way.

The only travelers he met there were a few pilgrims and a party of rich merchants surrounded by heavily armed guards. None had seen the lad.

It soon became obvious that there was no point in going farther. Nute could not have left the inn much before Thomas had, and, even taking into consideration that a boy of fifteen summers would run faster than a man over twice that, he knew he either should have caught up with him by now or seen him in the distance.

Nute had, quite simply, disappeared.

As he trudged back to the village, Thomas dreaded returning to the inn, explaining what had likely happened, and facing Signy's justified anger.

Signy might well be a living saint, but the dead ones were often known for their rages, outbursts that could make the earth itself shake. Even with that in mind, Thomas had underestimated her fury.

"Brother, I honor your vocation, your reputation in bringing felons to justice, and your healing service to the poor of this village." She pointed a finger at him. "But you had no right to involve my son in this matter without my permission!"

Thomas had no argument for that and bowed his head in humble concurrence.

"I had forbidden him to do anything further for Ralf, not only because of the inn, but I did not want his life put in danger. My lad and I quarreled enough over how he took time from the inn to serve the king's justice. That was between us, and perhaps you knew nothing of it, but common sense alone should have stopped you from involving a boy in a dangerous investigation. How could you?"

The very air sizzled with her ire.

"He said he would watch a man for me while I questioned other pilgrims. The lad observes well, and I wanted to know the man's reaction when he realized what I was doing and was approaching him to ask him questions."

She tilted her head and stared with disbelief.

"I did not ask him to do other than that. Truly!"

"Do you recall what young lads are like, Brother? Perhaps you were wiser at that age, but most are not. They long for adventure, never thinking of consequences. When the man left, all Nute could think about was making sure he did not escape. He would follow him, capture him, and bring him back. He would be a hero, and Ralf would praise him. Not once would Nute think that the man might have a knife or that the creature might see the boy following him, wait in a hidden place, and strangle him from behind." She slammed one fist into her palm. "Boys do not think, Brother! And you have encouraged him to endanger himself."

She had tears flowing, and her cheeks were as red from grief as anger.

Thomas's only hope was that this conversation must surely be coming to an end. He accepted his guilt for being a witless fool and readily confessed it. He not only understood her profound terror for Nute's safety, he shared it.

"I will go immediately to Prioress Eleanor," he said, "and tell her what has happened. I must beg permission to seek Nute on the way to Norwich, but she will surely grant it."

"Oh, indeed you will go to her now, Brother, and swiftly," the innkeeper snapped. "But it is I who shall get to her quarters first, for I need to speak to your prioress even more than you do!"

With that, the innkeeper raised the hem of her robe and raced toward the priory with the speed of a deer who had heard the howling of dogs.

Thomas did his best to keep pace with her.

CHAPTER TWENTY-EIGHT

Prioress Eleanor had never seen the innkeeper in such a state, not even when she had been bedded and humiliated by Crowner Ralf many years ago. As Signy explained the problem and why she was so angry, the prioress gave her monk a questioning frown. This was a rare lapse in his usually good judgment.

His return look was eloquent. It told her that he knew he was guilty as charged and deeply apologetic. His own worry over Nute was also evident.

She nodded without letting her expression reveal her opinion of what he had done. Although she understood why he had involved Nute and that he believed he had not endangered the youth, Eleanor agreed the innkeeper's worries were most valid. She would rebuke Brother Thomas in private, then forgive him because she knew he shared Signy's greatest fear.

Nute's life was in danger.

Her emotions now exhausted, Signy looked at Thomas, her eyes hooded with fatigue. "I beg forgiveness for my harsh words, Brother. In truth, I have no right to condemn you. I have also failed to stop him from following questionable paths that I could not anticipate." She threw her hands up with exasperation and turned back to

Eleanor. "But I fear for my boy's life! If he is following a murderer…"

"Seek out Brother Beorn immediately," Eleanor said to Thomas. "The two of you must find Nute before he suffers any injury. Much time has been wasted. We can only hope the lad has given up his quest and gone home by now, but do not tarry. Find him!"

Thomas nodded and rushed from the room.

Eleanor knew he had always been fond of the boy and had no doubt that he was as worried as she and the innkeeper over his safety. The inclusion of Brother Beorn in the search was not just to add two more eyes to the search. The lay brother was taller and stronger than most men. Brother Thomas looked like a battle-seasoned knight. The sight of two such men would cause most felons to drop any weapon and plead for the mercy of a hanging rather than what they imagined this pair might inflict on them were they angry enough to forget their vows.

As soon as the door to her audience chamber was shut, she urged the innkeeper to sit.

Gracia did not need to be told to bring ale.

Eleanor immediately sat on a bench next to Signy and gently took the woman's hand. "Nute is young, but he is not a fool," she said.

"But he wants to impress Ralf so he will make him one of his men." Signy began to weep again. "I will spare you another recitation of my plans for him to take over the inn, my lady, but I also do not want him to work for the king's justice because I fear he will be injured or killed."

"Ralf might be deeply flawed in many respects," Eleanor said, "but he loves the lad as much as you do. That has been obvious for years. Even when he sired his own sons, his affection never diminished. He would no more put Nute in danger than he would his little Fulke."

Her tears may have slowed, but Signy's expression still revealed doubt. She shook her head but could not continue.

Eleanor knew the subject of how careful Ralf would be with Nute was closed for now. She had sent two competent men to seek the lad and hopefully bring him safely home. Now she must appeal to the innkeeper's conscience on another matter, and she prayed Signy would be willing to help. She urged the woman to drink the ale Gracia had just poured.

"You might be able to help in this matter that Nute wanted to resolve. If you do so, the lad may lose his desire to pursue it."

Signy looked at Eleanor with both hope and confusion.

"What do you know of the man who was found murdered or any companions he might have had?"

"A bit, my lady. What innkeeper does not learn more than they ever speak about? Had Brother Thomas come to me first and asked, I might have told him, but today I was outside at the back of the inn, arguing with a farmer over his outrageous prices. When our good Brother came, he saw only Nute, and that may have been why he asked the boy for help instead."

Eleanor smiled at the innkeeper's attempt to excuse a man whom she respected now that she had calmed.

"The dead man was friendly enough when he sought quarters here. He told me he was a wool merchant from Norwich, accompanied by his servant, and explained he had gone on pilgrimage on behalf of his father, who had been a farmer. His father had died, and I understood there remained an unsettled quarrel between them. The merchant was quite moved by the holiness he felt at St. Walstan's shrine and was convinced the saint might even urge his dead father's soul to forgive him in return for less time in Purgatory."

Eleanor agreed that there was no end to what a saint might do on behalf of the ardent supplicant.

"There was another man who joined the pair not long after they arrived at the inn. I do not know who he was, and I was unsure whether he had any prior acquaintance with them. The three men often had meals together, and they seemed to have serious discussions. I assumed the subject dealt with some detail of faith."

"Did you overhear anything?"

Signy shook her head.

"What else can you tell me?"

"The morning the merchant's corpse was found, the third man paid what was owed and left."

Eleanor frowned. "Did he seem uneasy or in an unusual hurry?"

"He said that he had volunteered to find Ralf and send him back because his own home was on the coast." She thought for a moment. "No, I did not think he seemed uneasy but rather purposeful."

"Besides this one and the dead man, was there a servant?"

"Ah, now that is the odd part. I assumed from that man's demeanor and actions that he did serve the wool merchant, but I cannot swear to that. Perhaps he was simply a traveling companion." She pondered a moment, then waved her hand to dismiss that remark. "No, I did believe he was a servant, and yet he remained here after his master's death. He spoke with no one. I have no idea why he stayed. His room and board had been paid up for another week. I wondered if he was waiting for someone or for some message to come." She took a breath. "It was he who fled the inn while Brother Thomas was questioning others. It was he whom my son followed. I had seen him in his usual corner before that greedy farmer arrived, and he had disappeared when I came back to look for Nute."

Eleanor's fear for Nute's safety grew. If this servant was the killer and fled to avoid discovery by her monk, then the man might capture Nute and, if caught, use him as a hostage. Brother Thomas and Brother Beorn would be strong enough to overpower a man alone with a knife, but they would be far more cautious if that same man held a knife to the throat of the lad. Nor was there any certainty that the man would let Nute go free without harm if he lost all hope of safety himself or if the lad no longer served his purpose. Nute could identify him and probably his relationship to the dead man.

Signy could remember nothing more of interest and stood to leave, begging pardon for her rudeness in demanding she see Eleanor without so much as an explanation or an apology.

Eleanor quickly dismissed the innkeeper's concern, swore she had every right to require an audience and that she needed no permission to see her whenever she wished. Then she sent her back to the inn with encouraging words about Nute's safe return home.

As she stood at the window and watched the innkeeper hurry down the path toward the village, Eleanor wondered how any mother could bear the pain, not only of childbirth but watching her beloved children face all the dangers the world brought.

Then she turned to watch Gracia remove everything from the table to clean it and knew she did understand just how much the love of a child could hurt as well as the joy it brought.

CHAPTER TWENTY-NINE

Thomas and Beorn did not speak as they approached the first wooded area on the road to Norwich. The few travelers they had met coming in their direction had seen nothing unusual, especially a youth of Nute's description, a man alone, or even the pair of them together. No one, if they could do otherwise, traveled the king's roads alone or in a pair. Even the poor were in danger because everyone had at least something lawless men valued.

The sun had passed its highest spot, and the air was now sticky with heat. No breeze tempered it, and birdsong was minimal. When the two men entered the shade provided by the beech and oak, both noted that even the buzz and whir of insects was muted.

They studied the area around the brush, hoping to find evidence that someone might have pushed through the thick growth recently. Brother Beorn found broken twigs displaying green, moist wood. He gestured at Thomas, who felt the breaks, nodded, and the two men struggled deeper into the dusty brush.

With immense relief, in a tiny clearing they found Nute.

He was carefully tipping a wineskin full of liquid down a man's throat. The arms and legs of the latter were tightly bound with bands of ivy vines.

Thomas wanted to both weep with relief and laugh at the odd sight.

"And what have you here, lad?" Brother Beorn glared, an expression that meant little because it was his habitual look.

Nute spun around, spilling some of the liquid down his captive's cheeks. The lad's face was pale at the sound of the unexpected voice.

Thomas saw no color staining the captive's grimace and realized that Nute was giving the man water, not wine.

The moment he saw who was with the scowling lay brother, Nute grinned with inordinate joy. "I caught him, Brother Thomas!"

"This creature is a cutthroat! Release me, good monks!" The captive struggled to free himself, but ivy vines were not easily broken, especially when several were tightly wound together.

"I recognize you from the inn," Thomas said. "You are the servant of the murdered man."

"I have no reason to lie, but my service to the dead merchant is no crime. I was on my way back home when I was accosted by this…" he gestured at Nute with his head, "…this brute."

"He is the innkeeper's son," Brother Beorn said. For a man of few words and grim demeanor, his tone bordered on the amused.

"Then he is in league with outlaws. I fear for my life. Release me!"

Thomas walked over and took the wineskin from Nute's hand, sniffed, and waved the object at the man. "Outlaws don't bother to give a bound man water on a hot day. They would sooner cut his throat."

"I followed him into the forest, Brother," Nute said. "He didn't go far. I caught him as he squatted to relieve himself."

"And struck me down with a heavy object!"

Thomas smiled at the lad and tried not to laugh. The tale promised to be a humorous one.

"I did hit him with a branch," Nute said. "But not hard. He squealed and tried to crawl away. I grabbed him by the feet and whipped his hose around his legs."

"I demand justice! He attacked me."

"Crowner Ralf will listen to your version of what happened."

Thomas went to the man and examined his head. "What is your name?"

"You are hurting my wound!"

"A bare scratch. Your name?"

"Oseberne. Formerly a servant to Kenwrec, a merchant of Norwich. Ouch!"

Thomas had parted the man's hair and was peering at the wound. "I can confirm that the damage to your head is minor. A small lump. Some blood, but only because scalp wounds bleed freely even with scratches."

"You are a monk, not a physician," the man growled.

"He has learned about wounds caused by violence after many years of assisting Prioress Eleanor of Tyndal Priory in bringing murderers to justice." Brother Beorn stepped closer and peered down with narrowed eyes.

Oseberne squirmed under the malevolent gaze of the grim religious. "Then you know violence has been committed against me by this lout."

"And with good reason," Thomas replied. "Why did you flee the inn? You say you were returning home, but I have learned that you took none of your possessions with you and you still had a few more days paid at the inn. It takes about four hours to reach Norwich from here, and it is late in the day. Why travel now, alone and in the heat, when you could have gone earlier in the coolness of morning and likely in the safe company of others?"

"Have I committed a crime in doing any of that?"

"No, but it is an odd thing to leave so suddenly that you forget to take your possessions with you."

"Nor is it a crime to be forgetful."

Thomas shook his head. "When a murder has occurred, anything out of the usual is of interest."

"What right do you have to question me, Brother? You have no authority outside your priory. Your only proper act is to free me and let me be on my way. Take this monster home by the ear to his mother if you are so convinced he has done no harm worthy of a cell."

"To free you would anger Crowner Ralf, who will wish to question you, Oseberne. It was his request that I question anyone who was at the inn at the time your master was killed. Yet you fled before I could talk to you." Thomas's expression offered no sympathy. "Running away under such circumstances suggests to any rational man that the fugitive might have cause to escape, and that cause might be guilt."

"My master's death is not the business of the Church. Go back to your priory and pray for souls!"

"An excellent idea," Thomas replied. Both he and Brother Beorn yanked the man back on his feet. "We shall loosen your bonds enough so you can walk, and the three of us will escort you back to the village. A comfortable cell will be found, and you may wait until the king's man returns from the coast. Then I can return to our chapel and pay heed to those souls who deserve my prayers."

"You have no right—"

"At the request of the crowner, I do have that right. I am simply making sure you are available to answer his questions, for the king's law demands it." He grinned with evident pleasure. "And we are all good subjects of King Edward, are we not?"

While Brother Beorn retied the ivy vines around the man's feet so he could walk but not run, Thomas turned to Nute.

"What a clever idea to use ivy vines, lad! Crowner Ralf will be proud of you."

Now that Nute was safe, Thomas decided he was firmly back on the lad's side in the debate over whether he ought to be an innkeeper or a king's man.

But would Signy ever agree?

CHAPTER THIRTY

Ralf and his men crawled over the sharp rocks and into the tall grass on a hillock above the beach.

As he strained to see in the darkness, he hoped he had fooled any spy by pretending to discount the importance of this very small cache of wool hidden in the rocks. Few would think it unreasonable if he decided that the amount was too small for a group of smugglers to chance capture.

To add to the smuggler leader's confidence, he had shouted to his men that the tiny quantity might also have been left behind if the sailors had fled for some reason before everything had been picked up. Then he and his men had stomped off.

Ralf knew he lacked subtlety, but he hoped his reputation for blunt decisiveness had given greater credence to the quick dismissal he gave the few bales.

The light from the moon was dim, and the crowner's eyes ached as he strained to see any moving shadows of a boat or men below him. Although he had always had excellent vision at night, he knew his acuity had diminished in the last year. Yet another reason to mourn the loss of Warin, who could see a raven nesting in a tree during the darkest part of Satan's hours.

A sharp pain of sorrow made him wince. No one had seen Warin since he had left Tyndal village. Ralf knew of no family the man had left in Norwich, nor did he know of old friends from whom he might have sought news. Warin never talked much about his past. The only thing Ralf knew was that he had once been a mercenary. Since Ralf had never wanted to speak of the reasons he had fled England and sold his sword for pay and booty, he knew better than to ever ask the man questions. Warin's competence was all he needed to know.

What he feared most was that Warin had been killed. But by whom? Was it on the road back to the coast? Or was the man still alive? Had he discovered something important and decided, foolishly, to pursue the matter by himself? If Warin was dead, he would hunt the killer down and hang him. If Warin was alive and had been foolish, he would wring the man's neck first for causing him such worry and then welcome him back with a jack of ale.

Whatever the truth, the smugglers were still in business, although this current tiny wool cache suggested something had happened to disrupt the usual routine. Was this the result of what Warin had learned? Had he frightened them? Was the spy still watching?

Ralf was convinced there had been just one spy for the entire operation, not one per coastal village. With many, it was more likely Ralf would have caught at least one. Simplicity in an operation was far more effective, and this leader had not only managed to avoid discovery but kept the smugglers safe for a long time.

But was the sudden change in routine caused by a problem with the spy? Might he be dead or under surveillance by Warin?

Whatever the cause, Ralf suspected that tonight he would finally catch the miscreants. He almost smiled, but he had never been a man to delude himself with joy until he knew his plans were successful.

A man on his right poked Ralf in the ribs. "They're coming, Crowner."

In the distance, Ralf could hear the creaking, splashing oars over the sound of the sea breaking softly against the shore. When he saw the vague outline of a boat moving swiftly toward the beach, his heart beat faster.

He did not reply to the man who spoke, and his men were trained to not even twitch until he roared a command.

So far, there had been no torch raised to warn the approaching smugglers of their danger. The tension roiled his stomach.

The splashing stopped, and the shadow of the boat's prow was very close to shore. Ralf watched as several sailors leapt overboard and dragged the boat onto the beach. It appeared that two men stayed with the vessel while the others scurried to the rock where the wool had been hidden from sight.

Ralf waited until the smugglers were far enough from the water and easy escape.

"Now!"

§

The raid was successful. Even the two men guarding the boat had been caught. Ralf grinned like a boy petting a pup and promised his men that he would buy them all jacks of good ale after the prisoners had been locked up in Norwich Castle.

But as he looked down at a man sputtering and struggling while being tightly bound, he almost crowed like a cock at dawn. He had learned that the capture of this one was crucial.

The cursing smuggler was the chief of this infamous band, and Ralf now knew he was close to putting an end to his long search. When he arrested the ultimate leader of the operation, the king would be happy. He might even gift Ralf's brother, the sheriff, with a small farm or a few rents.

As for his own reward, Ralf would ask for nothing. He was not a poor man and had proudly earned everything he owned himself. But his eldest son was his brother's named heir. The richer Sir Fulke was, the wealthier little Fulke would one day be.

CHAPTER THIRTY-ONE

"You are clever, lad," Ralf said to the beaming Nute as they stood in the street not far from the castle. "How did you find me?"

"I met a party traveling from Norwich on my way from Tyndal village. The news that you had caught the smugglers was all they could talk about. When I learned that, I knew you would first bring the men here to the castle to chain them up. And if you were not here, someone could tell me where you might be found."

Ralf almost ruffled the lad's hair but caught himself in time. Nute was no longer a child, he reminded himself. Instead, he clapped him on the back as one man would another.

"But why were you sent and not another?" Ralf attempted to keep the concern out of his voice and tried to sound as if he had no worries. "I pray your journey here does not suggest illness has struck any of our loved ones or—"

"Only more good news! A man who may be able to help you with the murdered merchant has been caught, and Prioress Eleanor is holding him in relative comfort at the priory with a large lay brother in attendance," Nute said.

Ralf exhaled with relief. "I know the cell and can imagine which lay brother this might be." He did not doubt that the prioress would make sure the captive was securely confined no matter how decent the food or clean the straw. He urged Nute to continue.

"He was the dead man's servant and inexplicably remained behind until now. When Brother Thomas came to the inn and began questioning those who had stayed longer than usual, the man fled."

"And our valiant monk caught him?"

Nute's cheeks turned pink, and he could not look Ralf in the eye.

"Do not tell me that you chased him down yourself, lad! You swore you would not endanger yourself if you did anything on my behalf. That was our agreement."

"I saw no harm, Crowner! But I could not let him escape. There was no danger. I knew Brother Thomas would quickly realize neither the man nor I were still there and come after me."

"You left word with someone about your intent and the direction you were going?"

Nute shook his head.

Ralf looked heavenward. "May God forgive me," he muttered, "for Signy will surely not." Yet he was secretly proud of her foster son for showing both courage and initiative. That was something he would try not to say to the innkeeper, however, as it would do more to fuel her ire than calm it.

"It did not take the monk long to find me," Nute whispered.

"In time to capture the man himself?"

"Nay. It was I." The lad's whisper was even softer.

Ralf covered his eyes and inwardly groaned. Might Signy's friendship with his wife save him? Probably not, he decided in despair. The innkeeper would skewer, roast, and serve him up in the evening stew. Gytha had already used up all her credit on his behalf. Had it not been for her, Signy would have fed him to wolves years ago for his sins against her.

"In the woods. I tied him up with ivy vines."

"You did what?"

Nute repeated what he had done.

At least the youth had come to no harm, and Ralf had to admit that he had been ingenious. Yet they both must still face Signy, a woman who had once given such a skilled tongue-lashing to a dishonest merchant that a well-made whip would have been humiliated.

"Very well, Nute. I shall praise your courage, quick action, and fine wits, but I must also reprimand your failure to honor your word to me." He struggled to keep his voice calm and demeanor authoritative despite his terror of the innkeeper. "You and I will speak further about this, but you must burn this lesson into your heart now. A man's word is like a vow to God. If he breaks it, he is a scoundrel and unworthy of the company of honorable men."

"Yes, Crowner."

"You are young. You lack crucial experience. How can you act wisely when you do not know the possible dangers and consequences of actions such as the one you took in this matter? To be foolhardy leads to failure at best and tragedy at worst." Ralf carefully produced a stern scowl.

"Yes, Crowner."

"But surely your foster mother allowed you to seek me out, so perhaps she is not too angry?" Ralf knew this was wishful thinking, but he also didn't want to be too hard on Nute. Were God and Signy kind, the latter he sadly doubted, the youth could become a clever investigator of crimes. The lad was eager to learn and was both more thoughtful and careful by nature than most of his contemporaries.

"She did, Crowner." Nute grimaced as he remembered her barbed words and how it had been necessary for Prioress Eleanor to persuade his mother to let him come to Norwich. He did not know what promises had been made between the two women, for they had carefully moved too far away for him to hear and they spoke only in tense whispers.

"Did you learn anything from the servant?"

"Very little. He admitted that he was in the service of the dead merchant, but he refused to accept the authority of Brother Thomas and Brother Beorn. He claimed I was an outlaw and had accosted him on the road like any common felon." Nute hesitated. "I only hit him a little. Brother Thomas confirmed I had done but slight damage to the man's skull."

Ralf did not want to even imagine the potential legal problems with that, then decided he would find a way to avoid them on the lad's behalf and urged Nute to continue.

"He insisted that he be allowed to return home to Norwich and refused to say more. If he were to be treated rudely, he demanded that I be held accountable for my injury to him and claimed there was more proof that I had violated the law than that he had."

A cart came around a corner too quickly, and the barrels it hauled almost tipped over on them.

Ralf grabbed Nute and shoved him to safety.

The cart driver seemed oblivious to the near-miss and trundled on, also ignoring Ralf's curses.

"Tell me the rest, lad."

"Brother Thomas promised you would listen to all the details of the situation from everyone involved and that you would return soon to hear his plea. Meanwhile, he and Brother Beorn would take him to the priory, where he would be put in a guarded but comfortable room until you came back. The man protested. Brother Thomas explained that, whether or not he liked it, he must be locked up. He was the servant of the murdered man, had fled under questionable circumstances, and had refused to answer reasonable questions."

Ralf chuckled. "Brother Thomas should never have taken vows. He would have risen very high in the king's favor at court for his cleverness."

"He is a holy man," Nute protested.

"Aye, he is, lad, but never claims it."

That was a profound compliment from Ralf. Since Abbot Odo, a man fat in body but thin in integrity, was his brother, Ralf viewed most men who took vows with little respect.

"Did you find the man who was supposed to bring you the message about the merchant's murder?"

"No, nor have I found anyone who saw him after he left Tyndal village." Ralf must soon deal with this problem. As a former soldier, Warin should be able to take care of himself, but his failure to appear anywhere on the coast where they had been hunting smugglers was not a good sign. Were he one to gamble, he would lay coin on the conclusion that the man was dead.

Yet no one had sent word that a body had been found either. Perhaps he should consider that a good sign. Outlaws usually did not like to advertise their more violent crimes. Had a band of lawless men killed Warin for what little coin he had, they would probably have buried his body in the woods or left it where wild beasts could eat it. Barring a natural accident, a found body might mean someone was sending him a message that hunting smugglers was not without consequences. No word at all might also suggest Warin was still alive. But Ralf was too realistic to let himself believe that.

"Will we be returning soon to the village?" Nute looked hopeful.

"Immediately," Ralf said. At least that was an easy decision. "But I must take the smuggler chief with us in case he recognizes the servant you caught or even the merchant's body, although that has likely been buried by now. To take the man with us, I must choose a few more armed men for the journey." Then he grinned at the youth. "I fear you will have to ride a horse on the way home, Nute."

The lad's shout of joy was worth what Ralf would soon face from the boy's foster mother.

CHAPTER THIRTY-TWO

Isemay, the smuggler chief, was wise enough to know it was pointless to attempt an escape from Crowner Ralf and his armed guard. By the time he was marched into Tyndal village, he had also convinced himself that he was unlikely to be hanged for smuggling, even though he was the one directing the collection of wool from East Anglian beaches to safe ports on the Continent. He wasn't even sure if hanging was the penalty for the crime. But he was a cheerful sort and confident in his wits. As long as he kept calm, he was sure he could find a way to avoid the hangman or any other penalty of an especially unpleasant nature.

What he did not count on was finding the solution quite so quickly.

Oswin and the widow were walking slowly around the market square.

The fishmonger waved to them and asked after Oswin's health, offering prayers for his continued healing. As the couple strolled off, the merchant watched them for a moment with a sparkle in his eye. Although the carpenter was a stranger, most assumed he was a good man or the innkeeper would never have tolerated him. As for Mistress Hilde, she was well known, respected in the village, and deserved a little earthly happiness.

"As God wills it," the fishmonger murmured and turned to greet the baker's wife, who wanted his fine bass for her family's supper.

Oblivious to the merchant's speculation, Oswin and Mistress Hilde continued their amiable conversation, and he was pleased to note that he was gaining strength. When the sun warmed him and peace slipped into his soul, he found it increasingly difficult to remember he could not stay here.

It would be easy enough for him to do so. As a stranger, it would take time for the villagers to accept him, but the innkeeper had praised his work, and his skills were needed. The man who had destroyed his family was dead and the search for his killer seemingly abandoned. What was the likelihood that anyone from Norwich would come this way and recognize him? He had changed over the years. Surely he could live out what days God had allowed him in peace, and perhaps even…

He looked fondly at the widow beside him.

She saw his expression out of the corner of her eye, and her cheeks turned pink.

Suddenly, Oswin heard a commotion and looked down the road coming into the square, where he saw a large party of riders. When he saw the bound man in their midst, he cried out.

The widow put a hand on his arm. "Are you well? What has happened?"

Isemay stopped. "Crowner!"

The riders stared at him, then immediately edged their horses closer to the prisoner to keep him from fleeing. One leapt to the ground and grabbed the bound man by the arm lest he suffer any hope of escape.

"I am not running away!" Isemay shouted at Ralf. "I must speak with you privately without delay!"

Swinging himself quickly out of the saddle, Ralf immediately went over to the smuggler chief. "A confession? Information about your masters?"

"A deal. I know a man who has returned after abjuring the realm. If I lead you to him, you can take him for hanging. In return, I want a pardon for the crimes of which I have been accused."

"More than accused. Caught in the act," Ralf growled. "If you can help me capture the head of the smuggling operation, I might consider some plea for mercy. But what you are proposing is—"

"If a man is accused of breaking the commandment against murder but can name those who were equally guilty of the crime, he may be granted mercy for his own evildoing and allowed to abjure the realm. Is that not the law?"

"If all those he accuses are found guilty or confess," Ralf said, and his expression suggested he was quickly losing patience.

"Then surely I, against whom there is only the accusation of smuggling, might expect a pardon for pointing out a murderer, one who had already been found guilty of the crime and needs only to be hanged."

Oswin gently removed the widow's hand and walked toward the crowner's party of men.

"Wait!" The widow hurried after him. "What are you doing?"

He turned to her. "Go back to the inn," he said. "This is none of your affair." Then he stopped. "Nay, it is the business of the innkeeper. Bring her here immediately. The matter is urgent. But you..." He felt the pressure of tears in his eyes. "You? I beg you to remain within. Whatever happens here, I swear to you that I will proclaim the innocence of all who have welcomed me to this village, for no one had any way of knowing the truth. And you acted as any godly woman would, with kindness and mercy. My last thoughts will be a prayer to God that He smile on you and give you joy in life."

She stared at him, her expression shifting from disbelief to horror.

With great effort of will, Oswin turned his back on her and strode without hesitation toward the man who would hang him to save himself.

❧

Isemay gestured with his head at the approaching man. "I demand my rights, Crowner. Here comes a man who was accused of murder, adjured the realm, and has returned. According to the law, you may hang him now."

One of the crowner's men laughed. "How does a smuggler know so much about this particular king's law? Perhaps his list of crimes includes one greater than smuggling?"

"I have lawfully taken enough such men to the Continent when they needed a ship," Isemay snapped.

"Bind the smuggler's feet," Ralf said to the man holding the prisoner, although he believed Isemay's claim that he had no intention of fleeing, and went to meet the carpenter.

"Who are you?" Ralf saw no fear or defiance in the man's eyes, only resignation.

"My name is Oswin, my lord, a man you may remember from years ago who abjured the realm from Norwich for killing a man while drunk."

Abjurations were dramatic events, so Ralf did recall the case—and with cause. In truth, he had known few men, and fewer women, who had chosen to abjure the realm rather than be hanged. Not only was the journey to the coast a dangerous one, but finding a ship to take them to France was hard, as was life in a foreign land. Terrifying though hanging was, that death was faster than many believed they would suffer on the way to find a ship at the hands of outlaws, or from those who believed the verdict was too merciful, or by slow starvation if no work could be found on the Continent.

"I do," Ralf said. Out of the corner of his eye, he saw Signy rushing from the inn, accompanied by a village woman he knew to be a widow. "You know the penalty for anyone who comes back without being pardoned. Were you found innocent, or have you been pardoned by King Edward?"

"Neither, my lord."

Turning to point at Isemay, Ralf asked, "Do you recognize that man?"

Oswin almost smiled. "I do. If you have arrested him for bringing me home, I beg for his release. He did not know that he had agreed to give a condemned man passage when I paid him for a space on his ship."

"That is not his crime," Ralf replied.

"And if he pointed me out to lessen his punishment for another crime, I hope you will grant him mercy, for he was right to do so."

The widow, who now stood by the carpenter, turned pale. "My lord Crowner, this man is innocent of wrongdoing. He has worked in this village and done good service. There is not one of us who has a quarrel with him. Indeed, he was savagely beaten, and no one has been arrested for that crime."

"What is this about, Ralf?" Signy looked up at him with utter confusion.

"I am not quite sure myself," he murmured and then looked back at Oswin. "You do understand that you are condemning yourself to the hangman," Ralf said to him.

"I knew that was likely when I chose to come back."

"Tell your tale." This was such an unusual situation that he needed to know more. When he looked at Isemay, he saw that the smuggler was as shocked as he over Oswin's easy admission. Like Ralf, he had probably expected the carpenter to flee or at least protest his innocence. Why would he so willingly stretch his neck out for the hangman's noose when the forest was so near, outlaws would welcome him, or he would at least die quickly with an arrow in his back?

"Some of this you may recall from my trial, Crowner, but to explain is only fair to the innocent villagers who took me in out of kindness." Oswin looked around at the gathering crowd. "None of you are to blame in this. Compassion is never a sin."

"Tell your story, Oswin," Signy said, but her expression revealed sadness, not anger.

"I am from Norwich, a respected carpenter at one time, with a wife and a child. Although normally temperate in habit, I became drunk one night at the inn. Soon after I left, I passed out and when I awoke, I was lying in a ditch next to a bloody corpse. The stained knife was in my hand, and my clothes were spattered with blood as well. Yet I had no memory of what had happened. Horrified, I cried out, and a merchant I knew heard my voice and ran to my side. He urged me to seek sanctuary at the nearby church, confess my crime, and abjure the realm. It would be a fair punishment for a man, he argued, who had been otherwise law abiding."

As Oswin told the story, Ralf recalled more details. He had personally handed the man a small wooden cross, which the abjurer must carry, this one painted white, as well as a small amount of money for food on his way to the Continent. He had also sent a small escort to make sure the man did not escape into the forest and to prevent attack by those who did not agree with the abjuration process. Finally, he had given him the name of an honest ship owner who would take him on board but not force him to share quarters with cattle.

"The merchant swore that he would take care of my family until I could pay for them to come to me in France. When that day came, I sent money and instructions for their passage, but I received no word back. There was an inn in a nearby French town where all those who had abjured the realm came to seek work. When anyone from Norwich stopped there, I begged for news. No one had any knowledge of my family."

Ralf was beginning to suspect where the tale was leading. He glanced at Signy, who looked back with evident sorrow.

"After many months, I learned that my wife and daughter had been cast into the street after I left and soon died of poverty and a pestilence. The merchant had stolen the money I sent and let my dear ones die." Oswin turned away, tears flooding his eyes. "Not only did he swear to care for them, I had promised to repay him everything he had spent to do so."

The widow began to weep, and Signy wrapped a comforting arm around her.

"Why come back?" Ralf heard the anger in the man's voice and knew he would have done exactly the same if Gytha and their children had died like that. He also knew the answer Oswin would give him.

"To murder the man who killed my family." Oswin roughly brushed his cheeks dry. His voice was firm with quiet determination. "Who would convict the merchant for allowing my family to die like that? What proof could I find, and who would believe a man already charged with murder. Yet he had killed them, and I wanted justice. There was no point in begging God to forgive me. I was already a condemned man. If I went to Hell, I would at least burn knowing the deaths of my wife and child had been properly avenged."

Ralf frowned. "The merchant who was murdered here..." He stopped and waited for the man to speak.

"He was the man I came to kill."

"Oswin could not have done this crime!" The widow turned to the innkeeper. "You are able to confirm it. So can the priory lay brother who attended him after he was beaten. He was too weak!"

Ralf nodded to the carpenter. "What have you to say? You seem to be an honest man, despite the villainy for which you were convicted, and an admission would be a kindness to all. You cannot hang twice for separate crimes."

"I did not kill the merchant. I may be guilty of planning to do so. I regret I was not the one to kill him. Indeed, I saw him in the inn one day and fled, hoping he did not see me. My desire for revenge was so strong that sleep escaped me, which was why I was out the night I was beaten."

"Was it the merchant who attacked you?" Something was not quite right in this tale, Ralf thought.

"No." Oswin's smile was grim. "Kenwrec was the name of the one who destroyed my loved ones, a wool merchant in Norwich. But he would never sully his hands with such petty violence. He would order his servant, Oseberne, to do it. It was the servant who beat me. I recognized him right after the first blow fell."

"Did he mean to kill you?" Ralf imagined that the servant might have had reason to kill the merchant if he was ordered to kill the carpenter and his master demanded further villainies to remain silent on this one. If Kenwrec was a man of good repute, with enough witnesses to praise his virtues, then the servant would easily be found guilty of committing the felony for his own secret reasons.

"I wish he had," Oswin said. "But I doubt Kenwrec told him to do more than beat fear into me. Perhaps he meant to keep me from fleeing so he could report my return to you or some other king's man and let the hangman save him from any harm I might intend against him."

Ralf was unhappy. This news did not help identify the merchant's killer. It only made the problem less clear. "I am arresting you, Oswin of Norwich, for returning to the realm against the rules attached to the mercy granted when you abjured the realm." He looked over his shoulder and waved to one of his men.

"Wait!" Signy said.

Ralf turned back with surprise.

"This man is still healing from the beating. He cannot tolerate a cell without someone to care for him. You may have to hang him, Ralf, but hanging is the penalty, not death from illness or ill-care."

Looking at the two women standing in front of him, Ralf knew they were right. Some king's men would welcome the death of a prisoner before hanging, but Ralf believed a man should die according to the law, not ill-treatment. He also understood that the man's story had been compelling. Whatever his particular crime had been, to which he had readily confessed at the time, his family had died because of one man's greed. Ralf also knew, as Oswin had said, that the merchant would never have been found guilty of any crime.

"Very well," Ralf said. "He may return to his bed at the inn. You," he nodded to the widow, "may continue to care for him. I will assign a man to guard him."

CHAPTER THIRTY-THREE

As Eleanor listened to Ralf tell the carpenter's tale, she struggled to keep her expression grave and her mind dispassionate, but her frail woman's heart defeated stern resolve. Tears wet her cheeks, but she was in the company of friends, people who were like blood kin. Any perceived weakness was ignored.

Finished with Oswin's story, Ralf went on to another topic. "As for identifying the leader of the smuggling band, he was probably the merchant killed here. Isemay, the band chief, claims it was the wool merchant's servant who met with him and sent word about the locations for where the wool would be left for the smugglers."

"Did this Isemay identify Oseberne as both servant to the dead man and the contact with the smugglers?"

"He most certainly did!" Ralf laughed. "When I took him to the priory cell and held open the door to show him Oseberne, the servant screamed like a king's peacock. Isemay looked as pleased as the Devil's own imp and confirmed that the man was his contact and Kenwrec's servant."

"How has the smuggler chief been confined?" Thomas tried to guess where in the village there could be room. Ralf locked most of his caught felons in the keep in Norwich. Only rarely was confinement required here. Prioress Eleanor had the one cell. Tostig, Gytha's brother, provided a guard and room on the rare occasions when that was needed, but he was in London on business.

Ralf bowed his head in gratitude to the prioress. "Another old storage spot here has just been converted into a comfortable cell, albeit without light. The enclosures are close enough so they can shout curses at each other. I have been told that their words are so sharp that if they could be shot from trebuchets, King Edward would need nothing else to destroy Welsh castles."

Thomas thought he had heard a soft chuckle and glanced over at Gracia, who was standing by the audience chamber door with her eyes lowered like the humble, modest nun she was supposed to be. But he knew she had been listening to every word of their discussion. As he had cause to know, she had tragically lost all innocence years ago and understood the darker world better than anyone her age should. That she was now able to find amusement in human frailty was a credit to their prioress and the love she had found among many at the priory.

As if she had read his mind, Gracia peeked at him, flashed a mischievous grin, then instantly returned to the posture intended to make her seem invisible.

Her own composure regained, Eleanor folded her hands and rested her chin on them. "From what you have said, Ralf, you may have solved your smuggling crime. The merchant who died here was the leader. His servant, who acted as the contact between the band and the merchant, is in custody as are the sailors and their leader who took the wool to Continental markets." She paused. "Yet how do you explain the recent delivery of wool for Isemay and his crew to take away? Who killed the merchant? And what has happened to Warin?"

Shaking his head, Ralf said, "The last collection of wool was unusually small. That suggests that the delivery may have been arranged before the merchant's death, and perhaps nothing more was added because there was no longer anyone to collect it."

Eleanor nodded and waited for him to continue.

"Perhaps the servant killed the merchant over a dispute. As for

Warin, I must assume he has also been killed. No one has seen him since he left here to find me. No word has been sent either from him or on his behalf. His killer could be an outlaw or…" Ralf felt his throat go dry with both anger and sorrow. To avoid betraying his emotions, he shrugged.

"All this is possible," Eleanor replied, "but each unresolved detail raises troubling questions. If the servant killed his master, why remain so long at the inn? Someone paid his bill in advance so he might remain here. Was he waiting for directions from someone after this Kenwrec died? And where is Warin? If he was killed, which seems possible from what you just said, who did so? The servant was here. If he found a way to kill your man, how did he do it?"

"Concerns I share with you, my lady. I have yet to question Oseberne further."

"May I make a suggestion?" Eleanor smiled, for she and Ralf had worked together over too many years for either to mind such a thing.

"I welcome any questions, thoughts, or conclusions. I need to satisfy the king very soon that all things connected to the smuggling operation have been resolved."

And not just because justice must be served, Eleanor thought, noting the anxiety etched on her friend's face. He was worried about his wife and wanted to be with her.

"Were Brother Thomas to talk with Oseberne and offer some form of clemency for the truth and the names of those involved in this thievery of wool to avoid the king's levies, he may be more willing to do so," she said. "A monk will not put a noose around Oseberne's neck. He brings peace from God."

When Ralf started to speak, she begged a further word. "My suspicion is that he did not kill his master, but he does know much more about the smuggling."

"I cannot swear to save his life if he is a murderer."

"Nor do I suggest such a thing. A promise that you will urge leniency is sufficient. That much you can do?"

Ralf agreed.

She looked at Thomas. "Try to be vague about the nature of the mercy you suggest, Brother, but to offer at least the possibility of some sort is true."

Ralf scowled. "That leaves me with Isemay, the smuggler chief. He swears he knows nothing more than what he has already confessed. He also wants leniency because he unmasked Oswin as one who must be hanged because he returned after abjuring the realm. I am not sure if that is possible since the two crimes are different."

"Some mercy can surely be granted within the intent of the law of abjuration," Thomas said. "You and I can develop an argument if you decide he deserves it."

"The carpenter's story grieves me," Eleanor said. "Even though he killed a man, he swears he remembers nothing and committed the felony while drunk. The crime was not committed in anger or premeditation. And no man's family should suffer as his did."

"All his property would have reverted to the king," Ralf said. "Sometimes a wife owns something in her name, and that she may keep. Occasionally, if the abjurer is known to the king, he may grant some mercy by allowing the wife to keep enough to feed herself and any children. In this case, none of that applied."

"Yet under the rules of abjuring the realm, the felon's family is not condemned along with him or her?"

"Nay, but they might as well have been in this case," Ralf replied.

Eleanor's look of outrage would have made the Devil shiver.

"If you wish Brother Thomas to talk with Isemay as well as Oseberne, you have my permission," Ralf said.

Eleanor gestured to Gracia, who immediately left to bring food and ale. "And perhaps with Oswin?"

"Of course, my lady, but I do not see what that would do to help any cause."

"Nor do I, Ralf, but I find myself wondering why Isemay would offer to bring Oswin back to England when he might suffer more for that than smuggling were he caught. Surely the man knew there was something suspicious about the need for the journey. I assume Oswin did not disembark in a known port. That alone speaks of a wicked purpose. How many dangerous and illegal ventures would one ship captain take? And isn't it curious that the murdered Kenwrec, likely the smuggling leader, is also the man who stole money from the mouths of Oswin's family? I find that unusually odd coincidence worth pondering."

Ralf blinked.

Gracia put a mazer of ale into his hand.

"I will gladly speak with all three men, my lady," Thomas said, "and shall do so without delay." He stood.

With a smile, Eleanor gave him permission to leave, then turned back to the crowner. "Drink the ale and go back to Gytha and your children, Ralf." His eyes are half-shut with weariness, she thought, and I swear that his hair has a gray streak it did not have a month ago. "You have been too long from home."

With a grateful smile, the crowner downed his ale and quickly left her audience chamber.

CHAPTER THIRTY-FOUR

Oseberne stared at the monk with as much gladness as a fox cub might the sight of a circling eagle.

Ignoring the chill greeting, Thomas smiled.

The dead merchant's former servant still refused to participate in any ritual of courtesy, even to a religious.

"I bring God's peace."

"Freedom would be better received at this moment, Brother. I am falsely accused." The man emphasized his plea by rattling the chain that attached his leg to the stone wall.

"Shall I first offer some worldly advice?"

"I listen. Indeed, I fear I have no choice."

"If you did not murder your master, you would be well-advised to provide full details about his smuggling operation and any information leading to the capture of his true killer. For providing something that might stop future smuggling, you could receive a far lesser punishment for the crimes you have committed. The king grows weary with these evasions of his wool levies. Such acts are taking on the dark hue of treason."

In fact, Thomas had no knowledge of what King Edward might be thinking, nor had Ralf when he asked. But Thomas tried to avoid the sin of lying by concluding that any king would surely be inclined to think just as he had described. "Murderers die at the end of a rope," he added. "As for a traitor's death, you might conclude that the loss of your hands would be easier to endure."

Oseberne's face paled to an ugly gray. "I killed no one," he growled. "You have no evidence." He looked Thomas with growing anger. "Why would I kill Master Kenwrec? He was a good man. He paid me well, gave me his worn clothes, and never beat me. As for smuggling..." He paused, his lips still visibly trembling. "Why should you suspect him or me of that crime?"

Thomas begrudgingly gave the man credit for quickly pulling himself back from terror. "You and I are too old for children's games, Oseberne," he said, not unkindly, "nor are you unwise enough to assume the crowner here is witless. You are from Norwich and cannot claim ignorance of his reputation. Few king's men are as clever as Crowner Ralf, and none are more honest."

The servant raised one hand in surrender. "I presume I must conclude that there is proof my master was engaged in illegal activity. That does not mean I was or that I had any reason to kill him. I repeat that I am innocent of everything and must be freed. The creature who should be bound with these irons is the young miscreant who attacked me on my journey home."

Thomas took in a deep breath and struggled to retain objectivity. This man was irritating and arrogant, but he also did not know that the meeting with Isemay had been reported.

"We shall come back to the question of how deeply you were involved in your master's crime in a moment. As to your likely guilt in the murder of the merchant, please tell me why the crowner should take your word that you were never beaten and had no cause to kill. In crimes of violence against men of some rank, the law often finds that a disgruntled servant is the perpetrator." Thomas was not a strong believer in this conclusion, but letting Oseberne think he was might make the man talk.

"That is not true! Surely the man who returned from France is the one who killed him!"

Thomas raised an eyebrow. "Now I wonder why you would say that? Are you confessing to beating Oswin in the market square? Perhaps on your master's orders? How else would you know that the carpenter had abjured the realm so many years ago?"

Realizing he had said something he shouldn't have, the man shut his mouth but struggled to remain defiant.

"You have just proven to me that you were in your master's confidence and know much that would be of interest to Crowner Ralf. This also suggests that you may well have had cause to kill if you believed you had not been properly rewarded for your efforts on your master's behalf. Perhaps an argument ensued, and you—"

"Brother, I swear to you on my hopes of standing with the righteous on Judgment Day that I did not kill my master." Oseberne's voice now trembled.

"I have not taken your confession, but if you lie to me or any priest during that sacred moment, you will stand only at the right hand of Satan as you burn in the fires of Hell."

Whether or not the fate of his soul changed his mind, Oseberne dropped his gaze, suggesting he was beginning to consider cooperation. But despite that and his evident pallor, he had not lost all worldly concern. "What clemency might I receive?"

Thomas felt some compassion. The man was guilty of much, but he had met far more despicable scoundrels. "The details I cannot give you. I am only a humble servant of God, but Crowner Ralf has promised to urge leniency on the charge of smuggling should you provide information on the scheme. If you are found guilty of murder, however, no relief can be granted."

"Please, Brother! You must first look to the man who abjured the realm for the one guilty of that. He confessed to killing one man before. Why not conclude he was the one most likely to murder again?"

Thomas did not waste time explaining that Oswin had been so badly beaten that he was unlikely to have had the strength to kill the merchant. Oseberne was fully aware of what he had done before Nute chased him away. And although tempted to ask more about the old murder to which the carpenter had confessed, Thomas was not about to let the moment pass if the servant was ready to reveal substantial details about the smuggling.

"First, tell me about the smuggling. I will relay what you say both accurately and promptly to the crowner."

"What I know is little enough. It is true that my master was involved in smuggling wool out of England to avoid the king's tax. He purchased wool from other merchants, eager to also avoid the levy, but argued that he should pay less for their wool because he had expenses in getting the wool out of the country, which they did not. He always allowed them some better profit so they would be more likely to sell to him, but he was a clever man and kept his own costs lower than he admitted."

Thomas was no stranger to the vice of greed. As a bastard born, his mother most likely a servant lass but his father of high rank, he was familiar with both the lower classes and the highest ranked. Both suffered from avarice, but it was often a sin freely confessed. The merchant class, with what he perceived to be their penchant for secrecy from each other, including friends, was a group he did not understand.

"I assure you that the other merchants did not know how he actually got rid of the wool. Whatever they suspected, they showed wisdom enough never to ask questions."

How could they not? Thomas understood that asking might sometimes be dangerous, but as a boy, he had eavesdropped often enough when forbidden conversations were taking place that he couldn't imagine not wanting to know details of something secret. In his experience, it was far better to know than remain ignorant.

"What was your part in the smuggling?" Thomas decided that the man was resigned to telling the truth, if only to save his neck—or hand, or whatever the king's justice might deem an appropriate loss for his crime.

"I took the shipments to the places where the smugglers would pick them up. These were locations where there were caves or some other place to hide the bales." He winced and rubbed his fingers. "Once, I had to wrap each bale in cloth and bury them in the sand."

Thomas waited, but the man said nothing more. "Who alerted the men to come to certain locations?"

"About once each month, I would meet with Isemay at my master's orders and give him the information. But I was not involved in the receipt of any payment, nor do I know who was. Indeed, I was forced to obey my master, as all servants must. I was not the man in charge."

"Once Crowner Ralf began patrolling the coast, who alerted the smugglers to his presence? Did you find willing men in the village to spy on the king's men?"

Oseberne lifted his hands in dismay and then dropped them. "I am innocent of that as well. Obviously my master had others he trusted. Someone collected the money from the wool sales on the Continent. He must have had a man watch the crowner's men. There were times Master Kenwrec left the house without me. Perhaps it was then he met with his spy. Not once did he mention the man—or men. I do not know if he had many or only one." Oseberne frowned. "I would think Crowner Ralf would have caught at least one in the coastal villages if there had been many of them."

Well noted, Thomas thought. "Was your master the only leader of this scheme?"

The man blinked. This was a question he had apparently never asked himself. "I cannot say, Brother. I suppose it is possible."

"Why did you remain behind after your master's murder?"

"That seemed odd to me as well. After we left St.Walstan's shrine, he grew pensive, something he was not inclined to be. He told me that he might have to leave me for a short while at some point in the journey. If that occurred, he would give me coin to pay for my lodging until he returned or else he would pay the innkeeper until he could send me instructions on what to do. This was a practice he had followed on rare occasion, but then he was killed. I did not know what I should do, so I asked the innkeeper if my master had said anything to her about my lodgings. She told me he had paid her for several days, so I assumed I would receive instructions of some sort.

Yet the murder frightened me, and I began to worry when I received no word of any kind from anyone. That was why I finally decided to go back to Norwich."

"Perhaps," Thomas said, "but the exact timing seemed to have been determined when you saw me questioning others who had been at the inn at the time of his murder." Thomas tilted his head and gave Oseberne a look that let the servant know he should not presume he was a fool. "You feared you would be suspected of his death."

To the servant's credit, he said nothing and turned to stare with impressive concentration at a speck of straw on the ground.

"One last question before I leave you to speak with Crowner Ralf."

The man looked up with hope.

"No, you will not be released. I can only swear that your testimony will be taken into account in your sentencing."

"But if I am here, who is to run the legitimate wool business in Norwich? Who is to take orders and keep accounts?"

"Things that should have been set in place before your master's pilgrimage. There are always delays due to weather, accidents, illness…"

Thomas was sure the man cursed under his breath. "Who was the man who enjoyed your company so often at the inn before Master Kenwrec's death? What did the three of you talk about? Where did he go?"

"He was a man we met briefly on the way back from the festival, then spent more time with once we arrived at the inn. If he gave a name, he did so only to my master. The two of them were quite companionable. I had never met him before but assumed the fellow had something to do with the wool trade. They talked much of the new tax, the quality of this season's wool, and other such business matters. To be honest, I didn't listen half the time. At least the ale and food were good at this inn. I had something to distract me in my growing boredom." He fell silent.

"He was also a Norwich man, then?"

"His accent was right, and he knew a baker and a butcher there."

"When did he leave?"

Oseberne chewed on his lip for a moment. "I didn't see him leave." He pressed a finger on a spot that seemed to cause him discomfort. "Nor can I give you a precise day he left, but he was definitely gone before I went back to Norwich." He frowned. "Do not ask me where he lived in Norwich. He did not say. Indeed, he never uttered one word to me, but spoke only to my master after he sought our company here."

Thomas suspected that was all the man could tell him, but he asked a few more innocuous questions. When the replies only revealed what seemed to be honest enough ignorance, he rose.

Only now did Oseberne beg a blessing. His eyes suggested he did so eagerly.

Thomas gave it willingly.

As he left the cell, he doubted the servant had killed his master, although he never doubted he had had a significant part in the smuggling operation. Whatever the king might think, Thomas viewed what Oseberne had done as one of the minor crimes to which men were prone, ones that were less wicked because they were less violent. Murder to him had always felt like blasphemy. Were mortals not made in God's image?

CHAPTER THIRTY-FIVE

Sister Anne welcomed her prioress to the hospital with solemn courtesy.

"Take me to those most in need of God's comfort," Eleanor said and prayed she was capable of bringing it, although she never felt worthy.

The dying always feared the moment the soul fled their bodies, even if their faith was strong. In the hearts of the loving and gentle, there was unease that they had not followed the precepts of alms-giving and compassion well enough. As for those who had done much evil in their lives, they began to doubt that God had ever believed their confessed regret—and perhaps had reason. They may have fooled mortals and priests with their bluster and lies, but as Death held out his skeletal hand, they realized with icy certainty that God was never beguiled.

As she approached the beds of the suffering, Eleanor offered each a smile. Whatever her own sins, she represented the Queen of Heaven in this priory, and, for her time at the beds of the suffering, it did not matter that her body was made of the same clay as any other. Her longing to comfort surpassed that. The warmth of her expression might be their last sight on earth, and she wanted them to feel confidence that their souls would soon be embraced in love everlasting.

As the parents wept, Eleanor sometimes knelt to hold a child when its soul fled to the soft arms of angels. After so many years as head of this priory on the edge of Tyndal village, she also knew most of the adults. With some of the dying women, she held their hands and stroked their faces. She was not allowed to touch the men. Instead, she assured them of how temporal this agony was and that God would not allow them to suffer long. Indeed, she believed to her very core that God was kind and loved His creations despite His profound anger toward those who abused their fellows on earth out of cruelty or greed.

Sister Anne stood by and watched. Although she believed in dulling mortal pain with a little poppy juice to bring the ease of sleep, especially as one approached death, she admired her friend's ability to bring a different kind of peace. Many claimed that the infirmarian, Sister Christina, was a saint, and the suffering gained the ability to endure when she visited them in the hospital. But Sister Anne also knew that the dying were comforted when Prioress Eleanor spoke with them. Perhaps they sensed that she was more like them, blessed by God though she was, because her deep, melodious voice, as well as her soft touch, suggested the understanding of one possessed of more human spirit.

After this visit concluded, the two religious left the hospital and walked to the apothecary. The sub-infirmarian knew that silence was a kindness to her friend. Only one glance at Eleanor was needed to see how drained of strength she was.

Suddenly, Eleanor stopped and looked up at her companion. "Has Gytha come to you for advice?"

Sister Anne understood how many other questions were included in that one. To many, she might lie or at least try to hide the entire truth, but Eleanor was far too perceptive to be easily fooled. Yet this was a problem fraught with the potential for sin. Her physician father might have learned an answer that satisfied him, but she knew his logic was deemed suspect in the minds of many.

"Her health, as you saw, is fragile," she replied.

"She has always been strong, but I was shocked by her weakness. She could not walk any distance without stopping."

"I have had experience with women in her condition. Before we joined this religious order, my husband and I were approached by others, once strong and healthy, who suffered as Gytha does after many births and miscarriages. My father had a remedy that I told my husband was successful in bringing health back to several women. He realized it was an unorthodox treatment and spent many hours in prayer. After consulting a priest who told him that he had never heard of wild carrot and thus saw no harm in using it, my husband agreed that I could try it. He sent all women with this ailment to me. In time, it became clear that I had greater success than physicians in improving the health of more of them."

The prioress said nothing. She stared into the distance for a moment, then simply nodded.

As the pair walked into the apothecary, Sister Anne first stopped to answer a question from her assistant. Then she invited the prioress to follow her into a small room. She went immediately to a shelf with jars of various shapes, took one down, set it on the table, and removed the top.

"This is called wild carrot."

Eleanor peered into it. The content looked like dried weeds, but then many of the sub-infirmarian's cures did and were. "How does it treat the problem?"

"My father often studied the Greeks—not banned by the Church—and had other physicians to whom he turned for advice. Thus he discovered that this, if properly used and the woman is able to recover, can restore her humors and strength if she is weak from childbirth and miscarriage." Sister Anne hesitated and stared at the brown-and-white bits in the jar before looking back at her prioress. "In order for treatment to work, it takes patience and discipline. The woman must not quicken with child again for some time." She waited for a question or some response.

Eleanor asked nothing nor did her expression reveal her thoughts.

"I gave her careful instructions and told her to explain all to her husband. If they follow my directions carefully, he and Gytha should have several more healthy children in the future but with less danger to her health."

Her face still unreadable, Eleanor nodded.

Sister Anne wondered if she had said either too much or too little.

The prioress reached out and firmly resealed the jar of wild carrot.

Sister Anne realized that the discussion of the cure itself was equally closed.

"Did Gytha seem content?"

"She left much relieved."

"Then Ralf will be as well."

With that, the two women talked briefly of administrative matters before Eleanor left to return to her chambers.

But she did not go there directly, choosing instead to walk through the priory grounds, ostensibly checking on the gardens, beehives, fishponds, and fruit trees. It was her usual habit when she wanted a quiet time to think.

As Eleanor well knew, there were many manifestations of God's curse on Eve. A few were ones she had never experienced personally. But every time she suffered her courses, usually accompanied by such severe headaches that even dull winter daylight brought her excruciating agony, she was reminded of the first woman's sin and the penance required of all her daughters. Her own pain often drove her to her prie-dieu, where she told God, with great sincerity, how deeply she regretted Eve's transgression.

Although she understood the need for each woman to be reminded of Eve's role in losing Eden, there was one aspect of that eternal penance her woman's heart never quite accepted: her own mother's terrifying death in childbirth. It was one of two sins she confessed most often, and her confessor's inevitable answer was that she must spend more time praying to God for enlightenment. Yet the question continued to vex her.

In recent years, however, Eleanor's heart had grown troubled with yet another related problem. Even though she knew that she had not yet prayed enough for wisdom, she caught herself asking if it was possible that God's will had been somewhat misinterpreted.

That question was surely a sin, and she occasionally had to confess it, only to be told that the remedy was more fervent prayer. But God's demands that she help render His justice and the time required to keep her religious fed and clothed did limit the hours she could spend on her knees. In any case, understanding had never been granted, and she had always had difficulty accepting things without a satisfactory explanation. It was something she had shared with her aunt, Sister Beatrice, who had raised her.

Keeping her intellectual frailties as a woman in mind, she gazed up at the bounty the fruit trees were bearing as she mused over what Sister Anne had just told her. It was not just the words the sub-infirmarian had uttered, but their more complex meaning.

She trusted Sister Anne's medical expertise and compassion. Under her direction, the priory hospital was now famed for cures throughout the realm. Some might still say that a talented but humble monk must be the reason for the success, but most ignored whether the hand that passed them the potion was male or female as long as their suffering ceased. Nor had any successfully cast doubt on whether her skills were godly or satanic. The saintly Sister Christina supported her sub-infirmarian and proclaimed that Sister Anne spent many hours on her knees, praying to St. Luke the Physician for guidance.

If such was true, and the priory hospital continued to gain renown in the land, a saint must be guiding the sub-infirmarian. And saints did not tolerate wicked practices. So Eleanor decided it was not important whether or not she understood what wild carrot was or exactly how it worked. If her sub-infirmarian had used it before with success and her work at the hospital continued to be blessed with such success, all must be well.

The trees looked fruitful, the gardens were adequately watered, and the bees buzzed happily. Eleanor turned back to her chambers, and her mind drifted back to murder.

Soon Brother Thomas and Crowner Ralf would return with more

information and perhaps allow her to finally piece together the story behind the relationship of the dead merchant and Oswin, one she sensed had undisclosed and possibly pertinent ramifications.

But had those led to murder? And how could such a severely beaten man have the strength to kill the merchant? The merchant's death might more reasonably be the result of a falling out between two men over the spoils of smuggling.

But who?

Oseberne was the likely suspect there, accomplice to his master. But was there a third who perhaps remained in Norwich? Might Isemay, the smuggling ship's captain, be a link there? Or was the greater felon in this messy tale the cleverer one, a person who was an equal partner with the wool merchant in the smuggling and now remained hidden from them all and thus might escape justice?

CHAPTER THIRTY-SIX

Thomas nodded to the guard posted outside Oswin's place of confinement in Signy's old hut.

The man fought back a yawn, unlocked the door, and waved Thomas in.

When he entered, he was surprised to see the carpenter upright, a mazer of ale in his hand. Standing by his side stood his nurse with a troubled look.

At the sound of someone entering, she looked over her shoulder with a glare, but her eyes softened when she Thomas.

"I assume you wish me to leave, Brother."

"He did not come for my confession," Oswin said to her. "Otherwise, there are no secrets here. I know I shall hang." Then his lips twitched into a thin smile. "Before I do, how may I assist you, Brother?"

There was neither self-pity nor mockery in his tone, and Thomas felt sorrow for him despite the crime for which he had been convicted. "Tell me your whole tale," he said. "I do not know it."

"It is simple enough, Brother. I was a carpenter in Norwich, a man to whom God had given a lovely wife and a beautiful little girl. I was happy in my days and nights. One evening, I stopped by a local inn, and although I rarely drank much, the ale that night must have been stronger than usual. I recall staggering from the inn into the darkness but nothing more until the sun began to rise. I awoke with blood on my clothes and my own stained knife near my hand. To my horror, I also saw a dead body close by, viciously stabbed."

"Did you know the man? What do you remember of the fight?"

"Nothing of the fight at all. Even after all these years, I cannot tell you anything about it. As for the man, I did not know him either. From his clothes and calloused hands, he was a man like me. A simple fellow who labored hard for his bread."

"Then you had no quarrel with him?"

"None of which I was aware then or now. Nor can I imagine what could have happened between us to drive me to such choler." He paused as if he assumed he had said enough.

But Thomas told him to continue.

"As I stared in shock, a wool merchant, Master Kenwrec by name, came by and saw what had happened. I had done work for him. He knew I was a steady man and not prone to violence or hot temper. As a mercy, he urged me to seek sanctuary at the nearby church. He would send for the king's man. I could confess to the murder, beg to abjure the realm for the crime, and swear my oath never to return."

"Who was the king's man?"

"Crowner Ralf. He may not recall all the details of my situation now, but at the time he was kind and made sure my guards were both honest and fair. I was able to make it to port and board a ship without befalling any harm."

That was typical of Ralf, Thomas thought. Despite the requirement to provide guards on the journey, many abjurers went alone and were killed in route to the coast. It was not unusual for a guard to decide that a permitted stop in the bushes at the roadside due to a call of nature was excessive, especially if the abjurer had been lucky enough to acquire a tempting amount of alms on the journey. Sometimes relatives of the murdered man, angry at what they considered a far too merciful penalty, followed and got revenge by killing the abjurer. Any guards were either paid by the relatives to ignore the violence or to assist. Ralf made sure the exiles at least made it to the coast and kept any alms for payment to a ship's captain.

"And your family?"

Oswin drew back and initially greeted the question with silence. His face reddened, his eyes narrowed, and his voice dropped to a hiss. "Master Kenwrec swore that he would keep my family safe until they could cross to France and join me in exile. If I sent him money once I had work, he promised to set some aside for their voyage and give my wife the remaining for food and shelter. Anything he paid over that, I swore to repay."

"What happened to make you decide to return to England, knowing you would be hanged for murder if you were caught?"

"My wife could not read or write, but Master Kenwrec sent me messages from her. Then they stopped. I wrote the merchant. He never replied. I no longer had friends in Norwich. I was a felon. Neither my wife nor I had living kin. Thus I had no one to contact for news."

The murder the man had committed was a grievous crime, but Oswin cared about his family. That spoke well for him. And had Thomas been in the carpenter's place, he knew that he would have braved a noose to return given the circumstances.

"Just as I had given up hope, I met a man, arrived from Norwich, who told me my wife and child had died of a plague. They had been living on the streets, cold and hungry. My wife had been forced to sell herself—"

Mistress Hilde gasped.

He looked away, unable to speak further. Taking a deep breath, he again faced Thomas. "The merchant had lied. My darling ones died, believing that I had abandoned them." His face turned red with fury. "Put yourself in my place, Brother. Would you not return to seek vengeance against such a man? I would die happy on the gallows for the one crime I could remember."

"Then you did come back to kill Kenwrec."

"Singing with joy at the very thought."

"And if he was innocent?" Thomas knew well the dangers in the blindness of rage.

Oswin nodded and took a moment to calm himself before saying, "I would have listened to him but, I confess, with little patience. Perhaps it is well someone else killed him before I did."

"Then you claim innocence?"

"Why would I lie, Brother? I am a dead man waiting for the hangman. Why not confess to a murder I would have committed had I been able to do the deed?"

Thomas knew the man was telling the truth. There was no reason not to confess to the killing, and despite his previous crime, Oswin seemed to be what he said he was: a simple man who loved his family. And he had tried to support them out of love and duty despite a moment, utterly forgotten in the oblivion of drink, when he killed a man, quite possibly in a literally senseless fight.

"Who did murder Kenwrec, if not you?"

Oswin smiled sadly. "Why would I tell you? Whoever did it commands my gratitude and respect. If the merchant could steal food from a baby and allow two innocents to suffer torment without either care or protection until they died in sin and of deprivation, he was a monster beyond redemption."

"Even if you refuse to name him, and I am not the king's man so cannot compel you to answer, do you know or suspect who it was?"

"I do not. That I swear on the memory of my dead ones. Should I learn, I will not speak his name. That promise I also swear on the memory of my wife and babe, may God have mercy on their souls!"

"I shall pray daily for them as well," the widow said and laid a comforting hand on his arm.

The kindness in her voice melted his resolve. Oswin wept.

As if he were her own child, the widow silently took him into her arms, pressed his head down to the top of hers, and let him sob.

Thomas turned away to give them the dignity of privacy, walked to the tiny window, and opened the shutter to let a ray of light enter the room.

The outside air smelled of hot dust.

Where was the justice here, he wondered. Frustration at seeing no simple answer in this situation caused sharp anger to fill his heart.

Oswin had committed one of the gravest of sins, yet he showed a tenderness to his wife and child that any priest would call exemplary. The merchant, on the other hand, had gone on pilgrimage, lauded for his virtue by a crowd of well-wishers, yet he had stolen money and caused two innocents to die of neglect because of his greed.

Oswin had left England as punishment for his crime, then returned solely to avenge the cruel deaths of his wife and daughter. The merchant had suffered nothing, despite his crime, until someone killed him for a yet undiscovered reason. Did Oswin deserve hanging for his return under the circumstances? Was the merchant's death not justice?

If Thomas were forced to pick the more honorable man, he suspected he would point to the carpenter and beg mercy for him.

Closing his eyes, he pulled himself away from his anger and concentrated on Oswin's inability to forgive the merchant for what he had done, as Christians were bidden to do. Yet his soul remained in rebellion. God might demand that all forgive those who had injured them, but were there not some crimes for which forgiveness was impossible?

Thomas begged God to never let him again meet the man who had raped him in prison or the man who had castrated Durant. A simple knife to the heart would be too fast a death for the damage they had done. At least God had shown mercy to Oswin and let another kill the man who had committed such a vile crime against his loved ones.

Fearing his thoughts were growing blasphemous, he turned back to the carpenter.

The man seemed much calmer and sipped his ale.

The widow had left the hut.

"Can you tell me anything about the smuggling Master Kenwrec might have been involved in?" Thomas quickly folded his hands into his sleeves, as if he feared they might be stained with blood from his own murderous thoughts.

"If I could, I would. Before I left Norwich, the only thing I knew about him was that he was a wealthy man, paid what he owed, and gave good wages to those who did good work."

"Did you know that the man who gave you passage back home was a smuggler?"

Oswin shook his head. "When I grew angry after learning the tale of my family's fate and swore vengeance, the man who had given me the news said he knew someone who would bring me to England for a fee. I thanked him for his understanding, and he explained where to find him. I knew only the name of the ship, never the captain's name. Nor did I inquire. In return, the captain never asked my reasons for arriving at night or requesting a landing spot on a lonely part of the coast."

Thomas let the man's voice seep into his mind, where he let it resonate a moment. Deciding he believed the carpenter but had no further questions for now, he thanked Oswin and left.

"I am done, mistress," he said to the widow outside, then hesitated. "You are a good woman, and God will reward you in time," he added and hurried off before she could respond.

But I am no wiser than I was before I spoke with Oseberne and Oswin, he thought and bowed his head with melancholy all the way back to the priory.

CHAPTER THIRTY-SEVEN

As Eleanor listened to her monk's account of his interviews, she was suddenly distracted by an odd vision.

Looking at Brother Thomas, she saw him as an old man, even though she knew he was only in his middle years. There was no gray in his deep auburn hair, but his face was gaunt and his eyes sunken. When had he developed those deep furrows in his forehead and around his mouth, she asked herself. Was his hand trembling, or was that her imagination?

She blinked, and when her eyes opened, she realized he was simply weary, battered in spirit, and gaunt from fasting. But should God grant him a long life, she prayed he would have lines of merriment in his face and a dancing sparkle in his eye. And without embarrassment for once, she also hoped that he would retain that lush and vibrant hair he now owned.

Thomas was waiting for her response, but his expression showed he was confused by the intensity of her stare and her silence.

"You have yet to question Isemay, the smuggler," she quickly said.

"I have not yet done so, my lady. The day was growing late, and I wanted you to hear the testimony of the other two without delay."

"For that I thank you," she replied. Her monk was a proud man and would never admit that three interviews in a day were beyond his current strength. She longed to tell him to go to Sister Matilda, who would feed him well, and to sleep in peace, knowing that God would forgive him and that she would fight like a she-wolf on his behalf.

Instead, she said, "You were wise to leave the smuggler to the end and allow more time to question him. Despite what Ralf has said, I think Isemay has quite the untold tale to tell. Forcing it from him will require time and strength, even with your skills."

He humbly bowed his head at the compliment.

"Why do men not tell the whole story, even when it might be to their benefit to do so?"

Thomas was surprised by the question but answered quickly enough. "Most often the motive is their sworn loyalty to someone or else it is to protect a person who means more to them than any ease in the sentencing." He frowned for a moment. "Isemay hopes to earn some clemency for identifying Oswin, as he will likely get. Why say more if he doesn't have to?"

"Well noted, Brother. But to whom might he owe that special loyalty of which you spoke?"

"The man who hired him to take wool to France."

"But that man is dead."

"Do you think there was a partner in the venture?"

"There are too many unexplained oddities in this story not to wonder."

"Perhaps the merchant was merely a part, but not the leader of the operation?"

"That I cannot answer," she said after a brief hesitation. "The unnamed man may be the sole head or else both Kenwrec and he ran it. Perhaps they had a conflict about the business. Remember that we still do not know who killed the merchant and why. If we knew how the wool smuggling was run and owned, we might have a better idea who did commit the crime. Was it someone who came here to meet him but did not stay at the inn, and thus no one would have seen him? With so many pilgrims coming through the village, one more stranger would not be noted. Did he immediately flee, or did he remain? We also do not know what happened to Ralf's man after he left Tyndal. Was the killer watching him and realized he must stop him from telling his tale to our crowner?"

"But Isemay swears he knows nothing more. How can he be made to confess?"

Eleanor smiled. "Isemay may well get all he needs on earth from the king's justice. What he still needs, however, is God's mercy. We shall need Ralf's permission, Brother, but I think it is time that the smuggler captain be brought here to face the consequences in eternity if he does not tell the whole truth."

He looked doubtful.

"I need your instruction, Brother. Is lying not a grave sin?"

"Aquinas would agree, my lady, if the statement is made in variance with the mind or, in other words, with the belief that it is false. And scripture does say that a sin committed only in the heart is still a sin." He paused to think about that and felt a chill.

"But the gravity of the sin depends on the damage done to others, does it not?"

He nodded. "A false tale told only to amuse, one that hurts no one, may be ignored. A lie meant to hide a murderer is grave."

"And maintaining silence is a form of lying when deliberately done to protect wickedness?"

"Good arguments have been made that such is true, my lady, and thus the gravity of the silence reflects the seriousness of the unspoken sin. A man who lies or stays silent to save another from murder might be forgiven. A man doing the same to protect the murderer is a sinner."

She clapped her hands together in delight. "Good! Seek Ralf and tell him that we wish to bring Isemay here for a sermon this evening. Our crowner must hear it as well." She grinned. "Do tell Ralf that we really plan to urge the smuggler to fully confess but shall use God's authority, not the king's. With God's grace, we shall succeed. Our crowner must be here if we do."

"I shall go to Ralf now," Thomas said, then laughed, "although I may first tease him about his need to be enlightened before I reveal what we are really planning. As I understand the distinctions, that will be a forgivable lie, one intended to harmlessly entertain…"

She cheerfully shooed him off to seek the crowner, but the moment her door shut, she held a hand to her heart. How joyful it was to have heard him laugh.

CHAPTER THIRTY-EIGHT

The prioress's audience chamber that evening could have awed kings. Secular grandeur might require glittering jewels and opulent pageantry, but the Prioress of Tyndal also believed that the God of burning bushes and terrifying silence needed far less to set a mood.

Eleanor, veiled and simply robed, sat as straight as a church pillar in her raised, carved chair, her staff of office clasped firmly in her hand. The silver crook glittered in the light provided by flickering beeswax candles. These gave off a delicate scent of sweet honey that suggested the air a soul might breathe in Heaven.

On her right stood Sister Ruth, a bent old woman whose deeply grooved face and grim demeanor were graphic reminders to mortals of the wages of sin and the terrors of Hell.

On her left was the gentle Sister Anne, with a profoundly sorrowful expression. Her eyes were moist, as if begging God's children to avoid the tragic error of facing Him with willfully undeclared sins.

Crowner Ralf had chosen to remain in the shadows, as out of sight as he could be in such a small room.

Brother Thomas went to open the door to the chamber, then stepped aside as two men brought in the chained Isemay. Once the smuggler was inside, the monk returned to his place just behind Eleanor, folded his hands into his sleeve, and bowed his head.

When Isemay saw the stern Prioress of Tyndal, a woman blessed with a holy vision and renowned for her service to God's justice, he began to tremble.

She gazed down at the man with the gravity of a judge about to render sentence.

Isemay fell to his knees and whimpered. His chains clanked loudly.

Eleanor let him grovel for a moment, then gestured to the guards to lift the man to his feet.

Fighting off their hands, he cried out like a wounded animal. "My lady, forgive me! I am too wicked a man to be in the presence of one so graced by God. I did not come here willingly. I swear it!" He began to weep.

Thomas noticed her slight frown. It should never surprise her, he thought, that many had heard of that vision of the Holy Family she had had several years ago, but it invariably did. He knew she had planned this audience to remind Isemay of God's power and the sweetness of Heaven for the truly repentant, but she would never have made use of a vision she believed she was too unworthy to have ever received.

"Stand." Her voice was firm, but not cruel.

"I cannot," he pleaded. "Nor dare I look at you."

The brief silence was as heavy as the day's heat.

"If you cannot bear the presence of a humble woman who is one of the least of God's servants, how much worse will it be when your soul faces the terrible visage of an angry God? He forgives the repentant, but those who refuse to confess all their sins have only an eternity of hellfire as their reward. His finger will point to a filthy, wild-eyed demon who will come and grasp your soul with his horny claws—"

"Please, my lady! Have pity. How can I recall all my wicked deeds? I beg for mercy. Were you to speak for me, He would hear your blessed voice." Suddenly seeing Sister Ruth for the first time, Isemay howled in terror and flattened himself on the floor.

Eleanor hoped her former sub-prioress didn't conclude that he thought she was the aforementioned demon. When Sister Ruth had arrived, Eleanor realized she was beginning to suffer one of her frequent gout attacks. For all the nun's faults, she was dutiful and knew her prioress needed her here. With luck, this session would not last long and the poor woman could leave. Fortunately, Sister Ruth was purblind, and she had been growing increasingly deaf. One glance at the older woman confirmed that she probably had not heard Isemay and was still trying to focus on the man.

Looking back at the smuggler, the prioress reminded herself that he was hiding crucial facts. "I can do nothing if you refuse to fully reveal all your sins to Him. What little you chose to tell the king's man may satisfy earthly justice, but a rotten soul can never escape God."

"What more does He want from me?"

"The complete truth. You have pointed out the man whom you helped to return after he had abjured the realm. You were caught in the act of smuggling wool out of England on another's behalf to avoid the king's tax. You have, however, failed to confess why you did either."

Isemay keep his forehead on the floor and still would not look at her.

Eleanor also suspected he was wavering in his determination not to speak after his shock. "Raise you head and look me in the eye," she commanded. When he would not, she ordered one of the guards to force him to do so.

In spite of mewling like a frightened puppy, he did obey. "My men are innocent," he whispered. "Will you not beg mercy on their behalf?"

Thomas glanced quickly at his prioress and, reading her look in an instant, said sharply, "Innocent? They smuggled goods to avoid the king's law. One should call that treason."

Isemay's eyes flashed anger. "They are sailors, not thieves, Brother. The details of the cargo are of no importance to them. They are paid to preserve their own lives, those of their fellows on the sea, and any passengers who put their lives in their hands. Ask them. Not one could tell you why we sailed, only that we did. They followed my commands but know nothing of what happened to the wool once we were back in France. Release them. They may find work just as easily on ships bearing the king's goods and serve him well."

"Or return to thieving," Thomas said.

"Not if they are hired by honest men," Isemay retorted, but his tone lacked firmness.

Eleanor quietly sent Brother Thomas a message to desist.

He fell silent.

Her smile grim, she said to the smuggler, "You may barter with Crowner Ralf, but you still cannot barter with God." Yet it had pleased her that this ship's captain put his imprisoned sailors before himself in his plea for mercy. She could not ignore that charity, and her heart softened toward Isemay. "If your men are innocent as claimed," she said, "they will receive a fair hearing. You, however, have more crimes to face than they do."

He rose back up to his knees. His eyes blinked shut with weariness, then opened to look at her with sorrow.

Eleanor knew she had won at least one fight, and his decision to talk was made.

"My lady, what sins I have hidden were committed out of family loyalty. Would God not condemn me for disloyalty if I broke my oaths and spoke against a brother who raised me like a father and supported our mother, as well as our young sisters, like a good son?"

Surprised, she wavered, then regained her focus. "That one of whom you speak must face God with his own sins, just as you must rid your soul of yours. That is what God demands." She knew she was getting dangerously close to treading on the sole right of a priest to take confession and give absolution, something no woman could normally do. She most certainly could not promise forgiveness. Swiftly, she begged God to ignore her sin and judge her in the light of her true intent.

Isemay's jaw set again with stubborn determination, but his eyes also shifted just enough to suggest he was continuing to weaken.

"Let God remain the sole judge of your kinsman's soul and do not add the sin of lies, even by omission, to the list of your transgressions."

The man slumped and covered his face. When he looked up, he was weeping again. "Very well, my lady. The carpenter's return to England was deliberately made easy. The man who told him about his family's fate was sent to do just that. When the carpenter was over-heard vowing to seek vengeance, he was given my name as one who would take him back."

"And why was this done?" The answer was quickly becoming clear to Eleanor but she needed to hear it, as did Ralf, still hiding in the shadows.

"If the carpenter returned, he would seek out the wool merchant who had both wronged him and led the smugglers. The hope was that either the merchant would be killed by the carpenter or the carpenter would be killed by the merchant. If the latter, the merchant would be caught and hanged."

"And was it your brother who planned this?" With well-concealed excitement, she realized they had found the missing man who made all the loose ends come together.

"Aye," Isemay whispered. "With the merchant dead, he could take over the smuggling and gain the wealth he had always hoped for. Master Kenwrec was a farmer's son who became rich in commerce. My brother wanted no less for himself and had grown dissatisfied with the portion of the smuggling profits the merchant had given him. When he argued for more, Master Kenwrec laughed at him and refused."

"Where is your brother?" Eleanor realized that the hand holding her staff was sweating, and she almost lost her grip on it.

"We are all from Norwich, my lady. I can only assume he is there. Where, I cannot tell you. He would not have returned to our family home because he wanted to hide from our mother and young sisters how he supported them. Indeed, he pretended to others that he had no family to keep them safe and told our mother and sisters only that he was one of the king's men and stayed at the castle there."

From the shadows, the crowner uttered a curse.

"Your brother's name is?" Eleanor's question was unnecessary, but she needed witnesses to the answer.

"Warin," Isemay said, his voice filled with deep pain. "He has long been one of Crowner Ralf's men but served Master Kenwrec as a spy to keep the king's man from catching us when we picked up the bales of wool."

Eleanor raised a hand to beg Ralf not to come forward for at least a moment longer.

Isemay now willingly looked at her with sad eyes and murmured, "Will God forgive me now, my lady?"

Perhaps she had no right to say, she thought, but did so anyway. "He will surely grant you mercy."

Ralf came forward, knelt next to Isemay, and hissed in his ear.

Eleanor nervously looked over her shoulder at Brother Thomas.

"Despite his anger, our crowner will be fair," he murmured.

CHAPTER THIRTY-NINE

Ralf longed to push Oseberne out of the alley and toward the dead wool merchant's house, then leave him to face the consequences. Were the results of this trick not of the utmost importance, he might have. At least it made him happy to think he would.

"He will kill me," the servant said between clenched teeth that matched the pallor of his face.

"My men and I are here to make sure he doesn't," Ralf growled, "but I promise you that I will leave you to his less than tender mercies if you warn him or in any way disobey my orders." He gestured to a sullen man next to him. "You have your knife?"

The thick-necked, broad-shouldered fellow grunted with ursine assurance.

Ralf grinned. "Look as if you have no wits," he reminded the man, "listen carefully, and make sure this fool survives."

Although the creature looked like any dim-witted cutthroat who had barely escaped committing crimes worthy of the rope, Ralf knew otherwise. Without question, the man was a ruffian but only a petty one. Ralf had saved him from having his hand cut off for theft of a platter with the understanding that he work for the king. Behind the dull eyes, there was a sharp brain. As for listening carefully, Ralf was certain the man would. Of greater importance was his alertness to any danger that a successful thief must own. And Ralf knew from observation that the fellow was ready enough with a knife.

One of his men narrowed his eyes as he looked over Oseberne's protector. "What if Warin recognizes him?"

"And if he does? What is your concern?"

"Why would the merchant's servant have him by his side?"

The borrowed villain yawned.

"Who travels alone on the roads through forests filled with lawless men?" Ralf smiled. "Perhaps our Oseberne had enough money to hire one protector. There are men who hire themselves out, and our friend here has a formidable mien."

As Oseberne looked across the street to a place where he was certain he would die, he whimpered.

Ralf thumped his back with brittle mirth. "Courage! You were brazen enough to defy the anointed king. You can save yourself a few days with hungry dungeon rats by helping us capture Warin. And I want a confession from him." He shoved the man toward the door. "Now."

Oseberne's attendant grabbed the stumbling servant by the back of his cloak, jerked him upright, and thrust him forward.

The unlikely twosome slowly walked to the dead merchant's door.

Ralf hoped that Prioress Eleanor had been right and Warin was here. To his later dismay, Oseberne had also said it was likely the man knew where the merchant lived. But so many promising leads had come to nothing that Ralf feared another failure.

When the door opened at the first knock, Ralf worried they had been spotted or even overheard, but no one peered out to look around, nor could he see a face in the darkness behind that narrowly opened door.

As the two men squeezed inside and the door shut, Ralf shook off his concern and waved to his men to take their assigned positions. Each of the potential escape routes around the house was soon under guard. As his location, Ralf chose a place under a window with a broken shutter, where he hoped he could overhear the conversation.

For once in this long investigation, he was right.

"I did not expect to see you back here so soon!" The voice sounded annoyed.

Ralf fingered his knife hilt. That was most certainly Warin.

"I was forced to flee," Oseberne replied. "That monk and the innkeeper's brat were asking questions."

"You had received no message to leave the inn."

"What was I supposed to do if they questioned me?"

There was a long silence. "What is this man doing here?"

"Who travels alone through the forests outside Tyndal by himself?" Oseberne's voice trembled even to Ralf's ears. He uttered a silent curse at the man's cowardice but then decided Warin would know Oseberne well and might think his fearfulness typical.

"And who does not pay off the guard and then send him on his way once he enters the city walls?"

Ralf began to sweat. Was Oseberne capable of remaining calm with these questions?

"I didn't know if I would be followed?"

Another long silence.

"And why is that, good Oseberne?" Warin's tone was far too warm.

That worried Ralf.

"There was no reason for me to remain after Master Kenwrec's death! I was given no reason for my long stay should I be asked. The innkeeper's brat had seen the three of us there together. I would be a suspect in my master's death…"

"Have you been paid?"

In addressing Oseberne's guard, Warin's voice had shifted to a more friendly concern, which, Ralf knew, would not even fool a child. Oseberne had already said too much for a stranger's ear.

"Or has my cheap friend failed to give you your due?"

Ralf hoped the man would take the hint and leave. The cutthroat might be fast enough with a knife but that meant little if he were outnumbered. Although Ralf suspected no one else was in the room, he could not be sure, and he didn't dare trying to see.

He heard a low grunt that a suggested a dissatisfied concurrence.

"Then I shall pay you, and you can leave for whatever low inn you fancy in Norwich. If you do not know this place, I can direct you to one with women willing to do anything you want. For a man with needs, they are angels."

The cutthroat said something inaudible but with a questioning tone.

Ralf sent off a prayer that the guard could escape without harm. If he emerged with money, he might even let him—

There was a shout of pain, a thud, and then a man's laugh.

Warin's.

Oseberne wailed as if he had just lost someone he loved.

"You never were very clever," Warin replied.

"You killed him!"

"At least I honored my promise and gave him angels, Oseberne. You did not even pay the man."

"I had to bring him, Warin! What if someone followed me? I was afraid. You could have just paid him and let him go."

"As I just said, you are a witless fool. He had heard too much and might have decided he could earn a bit more if he spoke to the king's men." He snorted. "No one would have come after you if you had obeyed my orders."

"They were asking questions. I was in danger."

"As was I, yet I did not run away reeking of such obvious fear that wild dogs would have followed to hunt me down."

"You left with the blessing of those investigating the crime."

"I confess I wonder what you would have told them if pressured?" Warin let the question hang in the air for a moment, then added, "Or have you already? What did you tell them, Oseberne?"

"Nothing! I didn't say you had killed my master!"

"Ah, so it isn't a matter of you *wouldn't*. It was a matter of you *didn't*? That change of speech tells me that someone did question you after all."

"I told them nothing. I swear it. I didn't say you and my master had agreed to meet that night. I didn't say that you wanted a higher percentage of the smuggling revenue. I—"

"That is most fortunate, my good friend."

Oseberne screamed in pain.

"No, I shan't cut your tarse off just yet, only prick it a bit now, although I seem to have a problem finding it." Warin's voice dropped, and all feigned humor banished. "I have now killed both your master and your attending spy. You knew about the first, and you saw me do the second. But there is something you have never known, although from the look in your eyes, you may finally have realized it. I always planned on killing you."

"Now!" Ralf shouted, heard doors and shutters breaking, and hoped they were in time to prevent another murder.

CHAPTER FORTY

In telling the story of Warin's capture to Prioress Eleanor, Ralf admitted that his faith was not such that he normally believed in miracles. Only twice had he seen evidence that they existed. The first was when Gytha had agreed to marry him. The second was when Oseberne had avoided death.

"Not that the fool deserved God's grace. He is guilty of much, but he did find enough courage to lead Warin into a confession, heard by me, and adequate to hang the man. For that, I believe he can be forgiven for the assault he committed against the carpenter. He may have beaten Oswin, but the carpenter lived, and the want-wit fled the moment he heard Nute approach."

Eleanor raised an eyebrow, then decided not to suggest that Oseberne might have softened his eagerness in the beating to his own advantage. Ralf was probably right. The man had served justice well enough, and the carpenter was healing. His additional involvement in the smuggling was serious enough and a crime for which the king would likely wish a harsh penalty.

"Now that you have in custody the murderer of two men," she said, "what are you planning to do with Isemay and his smuggling crew?"

"I have sent a message to my brother that Isemay provided such valuable information that clemency should be granted and that his men were innocent and ought to be released. I gave him my word that the sailors were paid to sail the ship and knew nothing of what would happen to the cargo."

Eleanor smiled. "And he will believe this?"

Ralf snorted, but his expression revealed humor rather than annoyance. "He owes me several good turns. I have given the family at least one heir. I am also willing to stay here so that he may remain at the king's side and have more opportunity to promote family interests. The end of this especially outrageous example of wool smuggling on our coast will bring a smile to King Edward's face because he needs the levies on wool exports to pay for his castles. In return for the king's increased favor, my brother will gladly let a few sailors go and let me decide what to do about Isemay."

"And Warin?"

"He will hang, and I shall stand on the scaffold to watch him twitch. The last thing he hears on earth will be my laughter."

Although their faith required forgiveness, Eleanor understood there were times when betrayal or cruelty was beyond the ability of men to follow such teaching. Ralf may have grown gentler after his marriage to Gytha, but Warin had betrayed his oath to serve the king. Ralf often said that when a man's oath was a lie, chaos ruled and honest men suffered. As for the crowner's especial pleasure in the hanging, because Warin had made a fool of him for trusting him, that was a matter she felt was best handled by a priest.

"Yet it seems there is one more unrevealed matter remaining in this sad tale, my lady."

"And what is that?" Eleanor noted that her friend was troubled.

"Oseberne says there is another story to tell and begs for a pardon of all his crimes if he tells it."

Eleanor glanced over at Gracia, standing at the door, and gestured for her to bring ale to ease their throats.

Gracia immediately obeyed, but Eleanor noted that her eyes twinkled with interest. Although she should reprimand the girl for her obvious curiosity about worldly matters, she never would. When she had been caught committing the same transgression, her aunt had simply advised her to be more subtle in her disobedience. If, as expected, Eleanor was to one day lead a priory or an abbey, ignorance of earthly ways was foolish at best and dangerous at worst. In Gracia's case, however, there was no point in pretending that her virginal innocence must be protected. Hers had been destroyed years ago in a way that no child's ever should.

Embarrassed by her distracted musing, Eleanor turned back to Ralf and indicated she wanted to hear what he had to say while Gracia gathered food and drink. "What tale is this, and what have you decided?"

"I confess that I have brought him to the priory, as well as Oswin. They stand under guard outside the gates to these quarters. Oseberne insisted that he speak in your presence and with the carpenter here as well. Mistress Hilde swore her charge was strong enough but urged that she accompany him in case of need." He flushed, knowing full well that he had taken advantage of Eleanor's good nature. "I beg forgiveness for not sending word…"

Eleanor knew this must be a matter in which the crowner desperately needed her opinion. "Hush, Ralf," she said. "If justice is served, then I welcome the gathering, as you knew I would."

He nodded with evident gratitude.

She inclined her head toward the door. "Send for them all."

CHAPTER FORTY-ONE

Eleanor insisted that Oswin, pale and shaking from his walk, be seated on a high stool. The widow knelt next to him so he might whisper to her if he needed assistance.

Ralf, two lay brothers, and Oseberne's guard remained standing out of respect for the prioress.

Oseberne dropped to his knees, and all fell silent.

"My lady, I come to bring justice and to seek mercy. For what I reveal, I beg a blessing from you and clemency from King Edward."

"God always grants forgiveness and blessings to the truly repentant," Eleanor said. "Earthly justice is not within my authority."

"As for the king's justice, Oseberne, it is fair," Ralf said, "but our sovereign lord firmly believes in the rule of law. Tell your tale honestly, and I swear that your plea for a pardon will be heard. More than that, I cannot promise, for I am not the ultimate judge in the matter."

With evident disappointment and sadness, Oseberne considered what the crowner had said but then agreed to the terms. "Nonetheless, I continue in the hope that the importance of my information will touch King Edward's heart and he will grant me the mercy of which great princes are known." He turned and gestured toward the carpenter. "Isemay was correct in saying this Oswin had returned to England after abjuring the realm. For so doing, the carpenter faces the hangman."

The widow squeezed her eyes shut and pressed a hand to her mouth.

The carpenter sat without expression.

"Yet Oswin is innocent of the crime despite his confession that he killed a man during a drunken fight."

Oswin leaned back with shock. "How can that be possible? Were I innocent, I would not have awakened near a corpse, with blood on my clothes and a stained knife in my hand."

Oseberne turned to the crowner. "I must start my tale at the beginning."

"That you should," Ralf said, "and I shall let you tell it to the end unless I need clarification of details."

"As you know, my master was a wool smuggler and a clever man who skillfully hid his crimes. I confess that I knew of his smuggling and participated, albeit in very minor ways and only because I had no choice as his servant."

Eleanor willed herself not to look at Ralf. She had suspected Oseberne was good at diminishing his role in illegal acts. Now she was certain. She and the crowner could discuss this later, if need be, but now she resisted the temptation to interrupt.

"I believe that my master thought his crimes were secret, and Isemay, for example, never knew his name." Oseberne looked longingly at the pitcher of ale. "I was a good and faithful servant," he said with a poignant cough.

She may have found the man despicable, but Eleanor gestured for Gracia to take him a cup.

Downing the ale in one gulp, the former servant thanked her and continued. "There was a man, however, who had learned of the smuggling. I never learned how he did. Since he lived nearby, he may have seen something that led him to the conclusion that Master Kenwrec was involved in the crime. I do know that he approached my master once, and I overheard shouting behind closed doors. The man threatened to reveal what was going on unless he received a portion of the profits."

Gracia poured him more to drink.

He grinned at her, then blushed when her dress reminded him that she was a nun and not a serving wench whom he might charm.

Regaining composure, he went on. "The night of the murder, my master told the neighbor that he would meet him at a certain time and place to give him the first payment from recent profits. Although he had not asked me to accompany him, I was worried about my master's safety carrying a large sum of money at night on Norwich streets. I went after him but kept some distance."

"How were you armed?" Ralf looked down at his hand and worried at a small insect bite.

"None, my lord. I deemed it prudent. A man with a cudgel is likely to be stopped."

Ralf nodded.

"What I witnessed was my master stabbing the man, then dragging his corpse to a nearby ditch. That done, he went to the inn close by. I followed, but, since I feared for my own life because of what I had seen, I made sure he did not see me behind him. Once inside, he looked around at the customers and approached a serving wench, whispered in her ear, and sent her off. When she returned, he pretended to taste the drink. The inn was filled with merriment that night, so she was immediately distracted by a thirsty group nearby. My master poured something into the pitcher she still held and left."

"I do not understand," Oswin said.

"I do not know what he used, but I remained in the inn. The serving maid took the order to your table and quickly left to serve others. Your jack was empty, you poured most of the ale for yourself, and drank immediately."

"It was a warm night, as I recall," Oswin said.

"Soon after, you stood up and swayed as if drunk."

"I did not understand how so little ale could affect me so, but I knew I had drunk enough and decided to go home."

"Although I did not know you well, you had worked for my master and seemed a reliable man. I was also still horrified over the murder my master had just committed and wondered what he had poured into your ale. Now worried that you might be ill after whatever he had done, I followed you out of the inn. I kept my distance until you fell to the ground and did not move. Just as I was about to help you, I saw my master come out of the shadows and drag you to the ditch where the dead man lay."

"At no time did you ever think to seek a watchman and reveal that your master was a murderer and should be arrested?" Ralf reached out for a mazer that Gracia had put within his reach.

"My master was a wealthy man, someone of influence," Oseberne said. "If he countered my accusation with the story that he had come upon me fighting with the man and seen me kill him, which witness would most men believe, my lord? Kenwrec the wool merchant or Oseberne the servant?"

"Tell the rest of your tale."

"My master rubbed blood on your clothes, Oswin, smeared it on your knife, and then put the weapon near your hand. After that, he slipped into an alley and waited. When the sun rose, and you awoke to the horror of what you believed you had done, he emerged and advised you to confess and abjure the realm."

"Why wait to see what happened? Of what benefit was it to you, especially if you feared for your own life should Master Kenwrec discover you knew what he had done?" Ralf frowned.

"I am a simple man, my lord, and often foolish. I wanted to know the whole story."

"Or you hoped to blackmail him?"

"I confessed to being foolish, not stupid. I saw the likely reward when my master killed the first man who tried to extort money from him." He stopped as if gauging the crowner's reaction. "Instead, I hoped my knowledge would gain me enough time to escape if my master ever showed signs he wanted to murder me for what I knew of the smuggling. I was bigger and faster than he and not as likely to let him stab me without a fight. In the time it took him to find another to kill me, I planned to flee. And, as you heard, Warin did intend to do just that. My fear was reasonable."

Oswin struggled to his feet. "Your master swore that he would protect my family until I could send enough money for their passage to France. What happened to the funds I sent?"

"The money came," Oseberne said. "My master used it to buy more wool to smuggle. As for your family, he amused himself by walking by as your child grew weak with hunger and your wife whored for—"

"No!" Oswin covered his ears and spun away.

The widow reached out to comfort but drew back her hand with evident regret.

There was no relief in the rest of the servant's tale. "But Warin found a use for you. He sent the man who told you the terrible details of your family's fate, then directed you to his brother, Isemay, so you might return safely to England."

"Why?" Oswin shouted.

"Because Warin hoped you would kill my master and he could take over the entire smuggling business. He did not know that you were innocent of the murder to which you confessed and concluded that it made no difference if you hanged for one or two murders."

"Hanging is too kind a death for Warin," Ralf growled.

"This means that you are innocent of any crime," Eleanor said to Oswin, now breaking her silence for the first time.

"I remain condemned, my lady." The carpenter had collapsed back on his stool and held his head.

"Not if you receive the king's pardon," Ralf replied. He nodded at Oseberne. "I shall summon a clerk to take down your tale."

"This can be done now, when memory of what we have just heard is still fresh," Eleanor said and nodded to Gracia. "You have heard the story. On my table in my private chamber, near the accounting rolls, you will find parchment and sharpened quill. Write everything you remember, then come back with it for any correction and for witness. Is that acceptable, Ralf?"

He smiled with delight. "Few have Gracia's quick mind and accurate memory."

199

Sending the young woman off, Eleanor said, "It will not take her long. Practice using a quill is always wise, but she is skilled enough already."

"My wife's abilities are proof of how well you teach your young charges, my lady."

Oswin still looked miserable. "Even if I am eventually found innocent and pardoned, I might still be hanged at any time. I am here without permission and have broken the law. It is my duty to remain in France until my plea is heard and decided."

Ralf agreed. "I will not tell my brother that you are in England when I send the testimony to him to give to the king. Instead, I shall ask that King Edward pardon you and send the decree to me so I may call you back home to receive it in Norwich." He looked around at those present. "In the meantime, Oswin, you may stay here where you have employment with our innkeeper and have gained respect if not friendships."

"Isemay accused me of being a criminal in public."

Eleanor nodded. "And Isemay was a bound felon when he was brought by the king's men. His word is already suspect. I shall speak with Signy. She is revered amongst us all. If she says you have been found innocent of any crime, the village will ignore Isemay, and you may remain in peace."

"I must still earn my bread and have a roof over my head once I am finished with my work for Mistress Signy," Oswin said. "And I have little enough left to do for her."

"I think your skills would be welcomed here should you choose to remain. Tyndal village does not have any carpenter, let alone a skilled one." Eleanor glanced at the widow.

Oswin flushed and also looked to the widow. "Indeed, I would like to find a way to start a new life in Tyndal," he said with a soft smile.

Mistress Hilde glowed, revealing how comely she must once have been as a girl. "You may well find that possible," she said, "but I swear to you that, no matter what happens, your loved family will always remain in my prayers."

"A lay brother is waiting to help you go back to your bed next to the inn," Eleanor said to the carpenter.

Ralf sent a message with the lay brother for the guard assigned to the hut that he was relieved of duty and could join his fellows in the inn.

After they had left, Oseberne stood, his sad eyes begging the crowner to speak to his fate.

"I will beg for clemency," Ralf said. "Yet I cannot promise you will not suffer some punishment. I shall argue that your cooperation has proven your regret for your wrongdoing and your willingness to serve the king's law in the future. You have given evidence to save a wrongly accused man from death, added details to resolve crimes, and risked your life to help catch a murderer. Those are significant deeds."

Calling for one of his men, he ordered him to take Oseberne back to his comfortable cell.

As he and Eleanor waited for Gracia's return with the requested document, Eleanor asked, "What are the chances that Isemay and Oseberne will be pardoned or gain any relief for their crimes?"

Ralf shrugged. "My brother will conclude that the king should not be troubled with petty legal details when he has far greater problems troubling him. The news that one smuggler leader has been captured and his partner is dead will be deemed sufficient. Warin's execution will be as grim as possible and demonstrate how little tolerance the king has for those who try to evade his wool levies."

Or for those who break their oaths to English kings, Eleanor thought. King Edward never forgave those, whether mighty Welsh princes or the lowborn.

Ralf gave her a half smile. "So Ismay and Oseberne will suffer time in the company of hungry rats and their own feces while their fates remain unknown. That may be sufficient punishment for both. Should Sir Fulke fail to follow my suggestion that both ought to be pardoned, I may suffer a distraction and be careless about returning them to the Norwich keep or at least wait until after Warin is hanged to let them escape."

"You would free both?"

"Oseberne is a lying and vile scoundrel. He hid until now that he knew far more about his master's business and especially Warin's involvement. But he also risked his life to get Warin's confession for me. Had I been an instant slower, Warin would have killed him, yet he did not betray me in an attempt to save his life. He will find employment soon enough with another Norwich wool merchant, and I shall learn with whom. If another smuggling operation begins, or he forgets that other laws are to be obeyed, I will know where to look first and pounce faster."

Eleanor hoped the crowner would be less merciful when Oseberne did commit another crime, something she was certain he would do. She disagreed with Ralf's leniency with him now, but it was not her right to argue for a sterner punishment under the king's law. With further thought, she might even decide his way had merit.

"As for Isemay, I could use him in my own service for hunting down other smugglers and miscreants. In his way, he is honest enough and does what he is paid to do." He winced. "I must ask if he and Warin had different fathers. Certainly he is less villainous than his accursed brother."

Eleanor laughed. "I confess that Isemay is a rather appealing rogue. With him, your judgment is most fair, Ralf."

"You are kind in your compliment, my lady, but you know that I am capable of cruelty, selfishness, and injustice."

"You are a son of Adam, Ralf, yet you have been forgiven of your most egregious errors and served your penance."

"I continue to serve my penance," he replied without any hint of self-pity.

Indeed you shall, until the day of your death, for at least one of those sins, the prioress thought. "And Oswin?"

"I will remain silent about his presence on English soil, keep him safe, and hide him if need be. We have use for an honest man of his skills in the village. He could have both a home and possibly a wife here."

"A good woman who understands that some wounds can only heal when they are treated with reverence," Eleanor replied.

CHAPTER FORTY-TWO

At Prioress Eleanor's request, they gathered in the innkeeper's house.

No one spoke or moved while she went to a corner and uttered her quiet prayers.

The tension was sharp.

Although everyone here had held each other in mutual respect and even love for many years, each knew this was a quarrel that might have no resolution and was likely to cause a grievous and painful breach.

Eleanor finished begging God for wisdom, looked up, and stared at the pale and roughly wattled wall a moment longer.

As if this had given the others permission to do so, they now moved cautiously around the room as if their footsteps might break something fragile.

The innkeeper stood near the food and drink and solemnly offered anything that might be wished. Only Ralf accepted ale, hesitated, then reached for some cheese before fleeing her glare.

Ingerith partially hid behind her foster mother and watched everything Signy did.

Ralf positioned himself as far from the innkeeper as possible while Nute edged closer to the man who had been like a father to him.

When Eleanor turned around, she chose not to sit, although Signy had brought the only chair she owned for the prioress's comfort.

How grim they all look, Eleanor thought with sadness. This quarrel should not have been allowed to fester and cause such sorrow. She loved each one of them and, as one often did with friends, even found their irritating ways endearing. The attempts of the younger ones to take on responsibility touched her heart. Both Nute and his sister had been good children and would soon be good adults.

Although Ingerith had not yet reached nine summers, she had already picked up some of her mother's mannerisms: the hands folded against her stomach as her solemn eyes shifted around the room to make sure she saw anything that might be amiss or need tending. Nute stood as straight as an arrow and looked at Signy with somber respect while nervous sweat rolled through the down on his cheeks.

Meanwhile. Signy showed a rare discomfort, fussing with the food on the table and looking anywhere but at Ralf and Nute.

Ralf was gnawing on a piece of orange cheese with the determined focus of a hound eating his reward after a successful hunt.

Eleanor could no longer delay her effort to bring peace and nodded at Gracia, who immediately went to the door and stood there to prevent interruptions.

As if they were one, all simultaneously focused their eyes on the Prioress of Tyndal.

Eleanor turned to the innkeeper.

"Mistress Signy, I shall ask you first to explain your wishes in this matter. I know you love Nute, and he has always shown you the obedience and respect in the past that we each owe our earthly mothers."

The innkeeper raised her trembling chin, put an arm around Ingerith, and hugged her close. "He has. I have been most fortunate in both my children. God has been kind to me." She shot a glance at Nute that froze him with terror but was not, in fact, unkind.

Grateful that Signy had begun the discussion gently, Eleanor smiled to let the woman know how much she appreciated her effort, one she knew was costing her dear.

"As you all know," Signy said, "I am an unmarried woman who was bequeathed this inn by my uncle because he had no male heirs. For many reasons, I have chosen never to take a husband. My foster children shall be my heirs." Signy hesitated a moment, and then offered to pour ale for any who wanted it. When all murmured that they needed nothing more, she poured a little for herself and slowly sipped.

Eleanor suspected the innkeeper needed the time to compose herself and decide how best to phrase her remaining speech.

"I had hoped that Ingerith and Nute would share in the work of the business," Signy said. "Nute would own the inn, of course, but he loves his sister. I never doubted he would make sure she received what was fair of the profits."

She glanced at Ingerith, who smiled with that child's look of utter confidence, convinced that anything her mother did must be right.

"Although she is still very young, Ingerith has shown great interest in all aspects of the inn. It seems likely that she could be of great help to her brother until, as most women do, she marries."

To help her friend get through this painful process faster, Eleanor added, "And thus Nute must own the inn, for if she were to own it, in whole or in part, her husband would take her portion as his own."

Signy nodded. "Yes. I wanted Nute to hold the business in its entirety so that he could always make sure his sister was provided for, married or not." She looked at Ralf and briefly smiled. "Although God made Eve as a helpmate to Adam, and therefore she was owed kind respect while she remained virtuous, not all husbands are as compassionate to their wives as, for instance, our honored crowner is."

Her look was so gentle he stepped back in surprise.

"Were my daughter so unfortunate as to marry a cruel man, I wanted to make sure she would never starve or be without a roof because her husband misused the profits of the inn or drove her from her home."

Ingerith tilted her head and, with a grave expression far better suited to a much older woman, said, "Then I vow I shall never marry."

Signy kissed the top of her head. "I would never accept that oath, child. There are many good men in the world, and one may well win your heart. To discover such a husband is to find a treasure that no sensible woman would cast aside."

Struggling to ponder complexities beyond her age to grasp, Ingerith fell silent.

Eleanor was glad the girl didn't ask why she might still need protection even if her husband was not avaricious and cruel. Although Ingerith and Nute had come to Signy on the death of their natural parents, Ingerith had only been an infant and had no memory of them. Nute did, albeit vaguely. Death was not yet a vivid companion always walking by her side, and, as Eleanor well knew, good men as well as evil ones often died young.

Nute stared at his sister. A couple of heavy tears flowed down his cheeks, parting the sheen of sweat on his face.

"And if Nute does not take on the responsibility of the inn?" Eleanor knew the answer, but she wanted both Nute and Ralf to hear it. Nute might not be fully aware of the implications, but Ralf most certainly was. Both needed to keep the problems little Ingerith faced vividly in mind.

Signy drank a bit more ale before she replied. "The immediate problem, if he does not, is that Ingerith is too young to do more work at the inn. I have many things I need to teach her, but I cannot do so unless I have his help running the business. Only he is both old enough and experienced enough to do this. I might hire another, but Nute is my son, able to take responsibility, and would serve me well. Another would require supervision for which I do not have the time."

Eleanor admired how Signy was presenting her case. Although the innkeeper felt Nute had been selfish and had deeply hurt her, Eleanor sensed not the slightest hint of disapproval in her voice.

"None of us can say when Death will come," Signy said in a solemn tone. "If I die before Ingerith can take on the work of running the inn, and Nute refuses his help, the place must be sold. That leaves Ingerith without any other protection but the good will of her brother." She looked over at Nute with a grieving expression.

Nute looked down at his feet.

Having finished the cheese, Ralf was gnawing his finger.

"If I live long enough and can train Ingerith, even without Nute's help, then I could leave the inn to her alone, but that does nothing to solve the problems involved when she marries. And thus I have begged Nute to put aside his wish to become the crowner's man and take on the inn to protect his sister, whom he loves." She raised her hands to signify she was done.

Eleanor turned to Nute.

The lad was weeping. "I swear to you all that I meant no ill either to my sister or mother. For years, I willingly helped serve, scrub tables, sweep floors, and even, as I got older, remove men who drank too much, got into fights, or otherwise troubled the serving women and others. But I have recently discovered that I have a talent for solving crimes. I feel a calling for that work, one as strong as a monk might feel to serve God. I long to bring the king's justice to our land as one of the crowner's men." He turned first to Ralf and then to Eleanor. "Did I not prove my worth in this last matter?"

Instead of answering, Eleanor gestured to Ralf. "Please speak to that," she said. "And do so plainly, for this is not the time and place for well-meant lies."

Ralf chose to avoid Signy's eyes and Nute's tears by speaking directly to the prioress. "Nute is a clever lad with fine wits, and he did prove that after the wool merchant's murder by finding and capturing the servant. In truth, I would like to have him in my company. As you know, my sergeant, Cuthbert, has long wanted to put aside the work of chasing criminals and devote his days solely to the management of my estates. He never wanted to hunt criminals and also longs to spend more time with his wife and family. Taking on Nute would allow me to choose another sergeant amongst my men. I also need someone trustworthy to replace Warin."

Nute blushed over Ralf's praise, but his heart was clearly breaking. "Yet I know my duty," he said, turning first to the prioress and then to the innkeeper. "I will obey my beloved foster mother, as I should, and offer my protection to my sister, whom I cherish."

Even Signy, although she was profoundly grateful for Nute's words, seemed grieved that he must give up his hope of working for

Ralf. "If there were any other way, my boy, I would let you become a king's man. Not happily, for I would always own a mother's fear for the safety of her son, but I could take joy in your successes."

The silence in the room was heavy with both regret and resolve.

"I have a proposal," Eleanor said. "Might you all consider it?"

Ralf consented with an eagerness that hinted he would agree to anything she said to escape the pain in the room.

Eleanor suspected that the crowner was also offering up one of his rare pleas to God that He give her a solution to this dilemma. As much as he had always cared for Nute and would love to have him in his company, he still felt guilt over his treatment of Signy years ago.

Signy was the calmest, other than Ingerith, who was again trying to look like a miniature version of her foster mother. The innkeeper gave Eleanor a brief smile, then bent down and whispered to the girl, "Go to the inn and see if our cook needs help, child. This discussion may take time, and you know she needs to discuss with you what she plans for the next meal."

The child joyfully fled what she probably suspected, from their somber faces, was the advent of a typically dull adult conversation.

Nute struggled to look calm as he nodded concurrence to the prioress's question.

He has utterly failed to hide his worry, Eleanor thought, but she would never hurt his pride. For all his longing to become a man who viewed the world with reason, he was not yet successful, but Eleanor loved him for the attempt.

She turned her attention to the crowner. "Ralf, are there tasks that Nute could do that would not interfere with his working at the inn?"

The crowner thought for a moment, then brightened. "Unlike my other men, he is skilled with figures, and he can read. If Nute could do these things in my stead, I would be freed to deal with other matters." He stopped, then raised a hand. "Someone who is as observant as he and can reason as well as he does could learn things that might help prevent crimes as well. Many strangers stay at inns on their ways to commit crimes. He could alert me to troubling things he sees without ever leaving the inn or pausing in his tasks."

Eleanor then turned to Signy. "Might you allow Nute to do these things for our crowner? Would he have the time without slacking in his duties to you?"

"That might well be possible. I wouldn't even mind if he occasionally patrolled the village streets at night, when large numbers of strangers pass through as they did with the recent pilgrims, but he and I would have to agree on the times and plan so we could arrange the accommodation of both responsibilities."

Nute's eyes grew bright with gratitude.

Eleanor wondered if he was aware he still wept and then said, "May all therefore agree that during the time Signy needs to train Ingerith in how to run the inn, Nute must take on the responsibilities needed to allow his foster mother the time to do so and for his sister to gain competence? Where our crowner can give Nute work that does not interfere with that, may he do so?"

"As long as he first and honestly tells me about anything he wants my lad to do, my lady, and I give permission." For the first time, the innkeeper allowed emotion to show in her expression.

"I swear it," Ralf said.

"As Ingerith takes on more of the inn's work, Nute could spend more time with the king's men?" Eleanor knew she was now getting into the troubling part of her idea and was not certain how this would be received.

Signy looked hesitant.

"When God calls you to Heaven," Eleanor quickly said, "the inn should be given to Nute. Ingerith could continue to run it, but her brother would own it. If Ingerith does not marry, she would continue to run the inn and even inherit it should Nute die first. It would be her choice whether to sell or continue, as it has been for you, Signy."

"I agree, but—"

Eleanor begged permission to finish before Signy expressed her doubts.

The innkeeper nodded.

"In time, Nute will likely rise in the ranks of the king's men. He owns good wits and skills. As he gains experience, he will also acquire

PRISCILLA ROYAL

wisdom and the ability to judge other men. If his sister marries, Nute could hire a good man to run the inn while still keeping ownership. Should Ingerith die before he does, he could sell the business or bequeath it to one of her children or one of his. No matter what the circumstances, I have no doubt that he will make sure there is coin enough to feed, house, and clothe Ingerith as a loving brother should. That remains his first responsibility."

Nute nodded with gravity. "I vow it, my lady, and I would do nothing without seeking your advice or any person to whom you directed me."

For that, Eleanor thanked him and promised herself to do all she could to protect Ingerith or, when God took her own soul, prepare someone else to do so. Then she looked each of them in the eye and asked, "What think you all?"

There was silence, but Eleanor sensed that the tension had slipped out of the room.

Ralf went to Signy's side and whispered in her ear. After a moment, she put her hand on his shoulder and smiled.

"I think I can speak for us all, my lady," Ralf said. "We agree with your proposal."

Eleanor suddenly realized she had been holding her breath.

As Eleanor and Gracia left the village, a lay brother walking a proper distance behind to provide protection, Eleanor hoped what she had proposed would work. She, Ralf, and Signy could confer on details and should also include Nute, who must now become the man he wished to be. But what had been accomplished was at least the foundation of a way to deal with the problem without painfully unresolvable conflict.

As Eleanor well knew, Signy, Ralf, and Nute had no wish to fight with each other. They had simply been caught up in their fears and, like many fearful people, had built walls of stubbornness and defensive anger. Thankfully, they had not grown too rigid and so lost all reason that they could no longer see any place for compromise. With relief, she felt confident that each could achieve what was most desired while surrendering only minor things.

And I must now return to the priory and struggle with my own blindness and failures, she thought and stifled a groan.

There was so much she must face with a tranquil mind and heart. Prayer might eventually bring God's wisdom to her in spite of her own inner chaos, but other matters required an immediate solution and a clear mind with which to discover it.

As she looked at Gracia walking quietly by her side, her expression thoughtful and her eyes still sparkling with curiosity about all she had heard and seen, Eleanor knew the young woman would have many questions when they reached the quiet of the prioress's chambers.

As Gracia grew older, she asked Eleanor increasingly difficult ones, involving problems Eleanor welcomed but also struggled to answer. But her Aunt Beatrice had taught her to be honest if she didn't have a solution, how to seek it, and how to teach another to do so. These lessons, along with her own admission that she had flawed knowledge, was something she was passing on to the soon-to-be new nun beside her.

As the gray walls of the priory came into view, Eleanor took in a deep breath.

One of the greatest challenges she must confront was how best to deal with all the implications of Brother Thomas's sin. Whatever the Hermit of Tyndal had said to the monk after confession and the penance he required, she must find her own path to understanding, with God's help, and any decisions which ought to be made for the good of the priory. As its leader, that was her duty.

And in the silence of that moment, a quiet voice now whispered from her heart that perhaps she too would be well-advised to consult with the Anchoress Juliana.

AUTHOR NOTES

Before I get into a discussion of things pertinent to this book, I owe a long overdue apology to the Welsh and anyone of Welsh descent. In *Twice-Hanged Man,* I spelled *Llywelyn* as *Llewellyn.* Despite my English last name, I have no excuse because my DNA proudly includes ancestors from southwest Wales, and, although my father spelled his first name with only one "L," we all knew it should have had two. Mea culpa!

To many, the medieval era seems a brutal period when it came to punishments. A burglar might have his hand cut off. People actually died in the stocks, pelted with rocks, and the most horrible death to most of us was hanging, drawing, and quartering. Almost all executions were public. Crowds often considered them forms of entertainment and occasionally brought lunch for the family picnic as they enjoyed the tortured last minutes of the convicted.

But there was another side to medieval justice, one that suggests that not everyone frolicked in gore. There were the notorious trials by ordeal, in which hot irons were grasped, one walked barefooted over burning coals, and drowning proved an accused innocent. An interesting statistic, despite the likelihood of infection, loss of a body part, or death, shows that 70 percent of the participants survived and were found innocent. One theory for this suggests that the ordeal did not last very long and that many medievals actually disliked corporal punishment. I leave the arguments to the scholars, but I do find the 70 percent intriguing. The Fourth Lateran Council of 1215 formally ended Church blessing of these ordeals, much against the desires of most secular princes. Without God's blessing on the procedure, other forms of rendering justice became prevalent.

Jury trials grew common, but conviction rates were low, which again suggested a hesitancy amongst mortals to render judgments that were previously deemed God's right—especially where the death penalty was involved. Compared to the modern conviction rates in the USA, which tend to be well over 60 percent, the medieval ones were closer to 25 percent. Of those, more were eventually pardoned.

Although not universally liked, the right to abjure the realm was one form of punishment for murder that didn't involve the death penalty. It served a couple of significant purposes: it got rid of people deemed undesirable by the community and also avoided the problem of "twelve good men and true" hesitating to order a murderer to suffocate by the slow hanging method.

The penalty did not always involve the crime of murder but most often did. The killer fled to a church where he (or she) was given sanctuary for forty days. At the end of this time, the sheriff, or other person responsible for the king's justice, would hear the public confession plus desire to permanently leave England for the Continent. An oath was sworn on pain of death never to return unless pardoned or somehow found innocent. The felon's property was turned over to the king, a penitent's robe was provided as well as a wooden cross, and the abjurers were escorted to a port, where they sought a ship to take them to the Continent. A strict time schedule was set up to reach the designated port. Other than the need for privacy during "calls of nature," they were not allowed to leave the king's highway. Families were allowed to follow at their own expense, and there were places in the Continental port towns where abjurers congregated to find jobs or meet their families.

The process and rationale are fascinating, but I can't go into all the details here. Many are included in the story, and I have listed a book in the bibliography that explains far more about abjurers in both England and on the Continent.

There are a couple of issues in this story that some readers might feel are presented in too modern a way for the era. Since I am not a fan of historical books where the characters are just moderns dressed up for a costume party, I think it only fair to give you my reasons in those two significant areas.

The first raised eyebrow might come over the subject of birth control. The Church unquestionably condemned it, although Jews and Muslims were more lenient on the subject. One compiler of canon law went so far as to conclude that any attempt to prevent pregnancy was so "unnatural" that even the act of incest was more acceptable.

With such strong opinions and the power of religion behind the prohibition, why would any medieval Christian try to limit births?

The short answer is that people have always done so and always will for reasons important to them.

Ralf wasn't the only medieval husband who feared he might kill his beloved wife with one more pregnancy. History is full of examples, among the famous and within our own families, of men who never forgave themselves when their wives died in childbirth. If there was a way to keep this from happening, short of a very difficult abstinence, they would, and did, try it.

Many families were also poor. The argument that birth control was of less interest because more children were needed to work on the farm and that childhood mortality was high had validity. But parents have always been parents, and the death of any child is hard. How many parents reached their limit of grief after seeing too many babies die of starvation or other results of poverty?

Thus people did try to limit births for a variety of reasons. The best proof of how common the effort was is probably in the number of religious and medical texts known or written at the time that talk about both abortion and birth control. Why talk about it so much if it isn't a problem? What I find especially interesting is how often these texts, condemning the very practice, describe how to accomplish it with impressive detail.

Methods varied in effectiveness. Wearing the testicles of a weasel between the breasts or using pessaries of manure might not have been the best methods, or only effective because either was bound to put many couples quite out of the mood, but some herbs seem to have had some value. Wild carrot, also known as Queen Anne's Lace, is still used today by many who claim it is highly effective. The truth of that I leave to medical professionals, but I thought the longevity interesting enough to have Sister Anne recommend it.

But she was a nun. Would she have?

Sister Anne, like most people, had a "common faith," but she did not come to the priory with an ardent religious vocation. She came because her husband did, and it was one way she could remain near him while still practicing her apothecary craft. She has always been, first and foremost, a healer, trained by her father, a noted physician in his time. When questioned about other things she does that are against conventional wisdom, like washing her hands between patients, she finds justification that satisfies others—or others often do it for her—and the reason usually gives a nod to religion.

She is curious, observant, and willing to experiment like others of the medieval period, including doctors and midwives of the Christian faith. Had those men and women not questioned common medical practices and developed others they found more effective, medical science would never have continued to advance. Western medical knowledge didn't just leap from Greece and Rome to the Renaissance. Many Christian doctors came home from the Crusades with valuable ideas learned from the Muslims and Jews as well as their own battle-field experience.

The next eyebrow arch might occur over Brother John's reaction to Brother Thomas's sexual encounter with the merchant. In fact, the medieval definition of sodomy covered an immense number of sexual sins, including anything that didn't lead to procreation. Male/male or female/female sexual bonding was in the same category as hetero-sexual sexual positions deemed unacceptable by the Church. The punishments for it varied from era to era and often among religious commentators in the same time period.

In the late thirteenth century, the Church was growing rigidly conservative. Burning at the stake for men bedding their own sex had already occurred in Spain. By the next century, the French king enjoyed his own form of an orgy by burning Templars accused of this, although his motivation was likely more about getting the religious order's wealth than any religious conviction. With the devastation of the Black Death, and the growing loss of faith among Christians horrified by the survival of the wicked and the death of the good, the Church found many targets to blame for the terrible number of deaths. Not knowing that a microbe was to blame, they dragged out the usual suspects: sexual sinners, followers of unauthorized interpretations of the faith, and, of course, the Jews.

Brother John, a man who believed his sexual pleasure in marriage was so extreme that God punished him by letting his son die, has spent much time debating how to atone for sexual transgression. When he finds wisdom in the life of his Order of Fontevraud founder, he is no different from followers inspired by St. Benedict or St. Francis. To Brother John, the image of the blessed Robert of Arbrissel marching into a brothel, facing the overwhelming temptation of women, and emerging chaste while also saving the souls of several prostitutes would have awed him. The concept of facing your greatest demon and conquering it to save yourself as well as others is not unique to modern psychology.

As for Prioress Eleanor, she may accept the penance given her monk, but she must also deal with practical reality and her own feelings. What might the Church decide to do with Brother Thomas if the story of what happened between him and Lambard becomes known, what can she do to protect Brother Thomas, and how can she deal within her own heart and spirit with what he did? Stay tuned...

On another topic, some may ask if Ralf had the right to urge confession from the dying smuggler? Doing so did have a two-fold purpose. He obviously wanted information, but he was also acting within the guidelines of his faith. In the absence of a priest, a layman could take a dying man's confession, although he could not grant absolution. In the eleventh century, the Archbishop of Canterbury Lanfranc discussed this (*Libellus de celanda confessione*), saying that in the absence of a priest, one could confess to "an honest man" and, in the absence of such a person, to God directly. As a military man, Ralf would have been familiar with the common practice of battlefield confessions to whomever could hear them as the wounded grew closer to death.

Robert the Devil is a real book. It is a thirteenth-century French work by that prolific and most famous of all writers, Anonymous. I discovered it when a dear friend pointed the book out and asked: "Did you know about this one?" (As is often the case with books she finds, I hadn't.) Reading more about it, I discovered it remained quite influential over the centuries. Giacomo Meyerbeer used the tale of sin, extreme penance, and ultimate redemption as one of his operas in 1831. Eugene Scribe, the librettist, was better known to me as the author of many "well-made plays" in nineteenth-century French theater.

So many flesh-and-blood men of the thirteenth century have been named as possible inspirations for the man in the tale that it makes one wonder how busy Satan must have been in England and France. I won't list them and recommend reading the book, and introduction, instead. Personally, I am happy to accept it as simply a good story that proved the compassion of God to anyone who longed to become a decent person.

Edward I was perennially in need of money. His wars and all those impressive castles cost a lot. Having done his best to bleed the Jewish community dry, he looked around for another source of income, and his eye lit upon the export of wool to the Continent. Since it was a highly prized product, he decided to create a customs collection system and put a duty on all exports. Needless to say, this was not a popular decision with merchants, and where there is an impediment to what people want or need, circumvention will be found. Smuggling became quite popular. It also took time for the customs folks to figure out how to patrol and keep smuggling at bay along a very long coast.

Enforcement did not become even reasonably successful for some time, as Ralf's struggles illustrate.

St. Walstan is probably not a saint who immediately comes to mind for most. He is, however, the patron saint of farms as well as any who work on them. Born in either Bawburgh in Norfolk or Blythburgh in Suffolk to a wealthy couple (his mother paved the way by also becoming a saint), he gave everything up at age twelve to work as a poor farm laborer as a religious penance. Known for his virtue and faith, he died after seeing a vision while he was cutting hay on May 30, 1016. His body was taken to Bawburgh, where he was buried. At the three places the oxen carrying his corpse stopped, a spring emerged, including the well still visible at Bawburgh. During the medieval period, he was a popular saint as was his feast day, celebrated on May 30 at Bawburgh.

Bibliography

As always, I have included a list of books used to write this mystery, from which I learned much. The list may be short, but each is highly readable. May you find something here to enjoy!

From England to France: Felony and Exile in the High Middle Ages, by William Chester Jordan, Princeton University Press, 2015.

Robert the Devil: The First Modern English Translation of Robert le Diable, an Anonymous French Romance of the Thirteenth Century, translated by Samuel N. Rosenberg, Pennsylvania State University Press, 2018.

Sexuality in Medieval Europe: Doing Unto Others, Ruth Mazo Karras, Routledge, 2005.

If you want further information about my books or would like to contact me, please visit my website at https://priscillaroyal.com or follow me on Facebook

ACKNOWLEDGMENTS

Patrick Hoi Yan Cheung, Peter Goodhugh, Maddee James, Henie Lentz, M. Louisa Locke, Paula Mildenhall, Sharon Kay Penman, Barbara Peters (Poisoned Pen Bookstore, Scottsdale, AZ), Jenny Quinlan, Robert Rosenwald and all the staff at the Poisoned Pen Press with gratitude for a wonderful publishing experience, Marianne Silva, Lyn and Michael Speakman.

OTHER BOOKS BY AUTHOR

Wine of Violence

Tyrant of the Mind

Sorrow Without End

Justice for the Damned

Forsaken Soul

Chambers of Death

Valley of Dry Bones

A Killing Season

The Sanctity of Hate

Covenant of Hell

Satan's Lullaby

Land of Shadows

The Proud Sinner

Wild Justice

Elegy to Murder

If you want further information about my books or would like to contact me, please visit my website at https://priscillaroyal.com or follow me on Facebook

Printed in Great Britain
by Amazon

78581877R00132